MW01120456

THE COMING OF ARABELLA

JOANNE GUIDOCCIO

SOUL MATE PUBLISHING

New York

F
GUI

loca author

THE COMING OF ARABELLA

Copyright©2015

JOANNE GUIDOCCIO

Cover Design by Melody A. Pond

Published in the United States of America by
Soul Mate Publishing
P.O. Box 24
Macedon, New York, 14502

ISBN: 978-1-68291-010-8

ebook ISBN: 978-1-61935-910-9

www.SoulMatePublishing.com

3 3281 02008 491 6

The publisher does not have any control over and does not assume any responsibility for author or third-party websites or their content.

To my beautiful nieces

Christina, Deanna, Olivia, Ava

Acknowledgements

To my family—Tony, Augy, Ernie, Judy, Lilly, Joan, Christina, Deanna, Olivia, and Ava. Thank you for your ongoing support and encouragement.

To the wonderful companions on my journey, especially Patricia Anderson, Carla Barnes, Fil Derewianko, Sandy and Jim Hill, Brenda McGinnis, Magda Viehover, and Cathy Whyte.

To my fellow toastmasters in Guelph. Thank you for inspiring and motivating me to continue with my creative endeavors.

To Editor Ramona DeFelice Long. I appreciate your professionalism and wonderful insights. Molte grazie!

To graphic designer Erynn Hayden. I'm thrilled with the promotional items you created for The Coming of Arabella.

To Senior Editor Debby Gilbert and the dedicated staff at Soul Mate Publishing. Thank you for making this book possible.

CHAPTER 1

Barbara smiled at the look of rapture on Belinda's face as she ate the last of the French fries. Impeccably dressed in head-to-toe winter white, Belinda continued to drown the fries in ketchup, not giving a single thought to any possible mishap. Socialite and philanthropist. Polished and playful. Assertive and flirtatious. Belinda Armstrong possessed that chameleon ability to adapt and thrive in any earthly circumstance. Today, she had regressed back to the behavior that had once helped her transition from mermaid to executive wife.

Belinda often reminisced about those extra-long days during her first Canadian winter. If the snowbanks weren't too high, she would walk over to the Carden Inn and order the fried and well-seasoned potatoes on the luncheon menu. Over the years, different chefs had come and gone, introducing healthier sweet potato versions, but the usually fastidious and well-disciplined Belinda would not even consider them.

"What would your New York friends say if they could see you now?" Barbara asked.

"I'm safe enough here." Belinda shrugged. "And even if a photo did get out, it wouldn't be the end of the world."

Barbara wondered if she would ever feel that self-assured. While she had made considerable progress during her own first year, she still second-guessed herself. But then her arrival on Earth had been so different from Belinda's. As Barbara started to recall those dark hours on the fog-drenched shores of southwest England, she was distracted by an overpowering odor of onions and garlic. Barbara sneezed several times as she reached for tissues in her purse.

Belinda frowned. "I hope you're not coming down with a cold."

"It's that smell."

"What smell?"

"Onions and garlic." Barbara paused, recognizing the warning. When she had requested Intuition as her third Specialist Skill, she assumed that it would manifest itself in other ways. Bright lights. Angel voices. Birds and butterflies. Instead, for the past month, it had been scents, and until today, pleasant scents.

The morning that Graham had proposed, she woke up to the glorious scent of roses. That evening, he had given her a large bouquet of red roses along with a beautiful diamond ring. Hours before she received her first raise at Eagle Vision, sweet peppermint smells tickled her nostrils.

"I don't know why you requested Intuition," Belinda said. "If only you had talked it over with me."

"And what did you select as your Skills?"

"*Touché*!" Belinda laughed. "I went with Makeup Application, Decorating Sense, and Dancing." She held up her hands. "I know. I know. Not the most enlightened of choices, but what can I say. I was young and foolish at twenty-five. Now if I had to choose at *your* age, I would choose very differently."

Barbara winced. It still rankled that she had started her human life without the benefit of her youth. As for her other choices, she did not regret selecting Cuisine and Public Speaking as Specialist Skills. But it was unlike Belinda to have any regrets. Barbara leaned closer. "What would you ask for now?"

"Financial Acumen." Belinda sat up straighter. "I would want to understand money like the Warren Buffets of the world."

It was the first time Belinda had ever expressed any interest in financial matters. As Barbara watched the changing expressions on Belinda's face, she realized the crux of the matter. Paul Armstrong was thirty-two years older than Belinda, and he would probably die first, leaving her a very wealthy widow. But she would have to depend upon others to handle her financial affairs. Barbara suspected Belinda paid little attention to any statements or accounts beyond writing checks and using her plastic.

Belinda squeezed Barbara's hand. "Enough of this gloomy talk. You'll feel much better once you sit down and have the conversation with Graham."

"I should have listened to you and leveled with him in March."

"But you didn't," Belinda said. "So let it go."

An eerie, buzzing noise startled both women. Everyone in the restaurant stopped speaking, and the waiters huddled together near the entrance. One of the chefs came out of the kitchen and headed toward the waiters. The noise continued for almost a minute and then abruptly stopped.

"The aliens have landed," the man at the next table joked.

Everyone laughed and resumed speaking. The chef went back to the kitchen, and the waiters resumed their tasks.

"Wonder what that was?" Barbara's voice quavered.

But Belinda wasn't listening. Her right hand trembled as she glanced down at her phone. She flashed the phone at Barbara, who gasped when she read the short message: *Mermaid arriving in Carden. En route from Toronto.*

Belinda grabbed Barbara's arm. "You must contact Graham at once. Before she arrives."

"He's somewhere on the highway between Windsor and here. I can't tell him everything over the phone." Barbara thought back to the previous morning when she had awakened to the tickle of a beautiful red rose. As soon as she opened her eyes, Graham kissed her passionately and apologized once more for leaving her with the last-minute details of the engagement party, but it couldn't be helped. One of his clients had expressed interest in a series of paintings, and Graham was anxious to close the sale.

"You must tell him before she arrives," Belinda said sharply.

"Who is she?"

"She could be anyone from the tribe, anyone at all." Belinda threw the phone into her purse.

"That strange sound came from your phone?"

"That's how the underwater Kingdom communicates with me." Belinda drummed her fingers on the table. "Usually, I get more details, but—"

Barbara wondered about the phone that could easily have been purchased on Earth. Like all other digital devices from the mermaid Kingdom, it did not stand out in any way. She wondered if any other ex-mermaids had such a phone but quickly dismissed that possibility. Unlike Belinda, they were not Bellas so it wouldn't make sense to entrust them with a direct link to the Kingdom.

"It may not be so bad," Barbara said. "It might be nice to have another ex-mermaid in our midst."

"You're making the assumption that she will be pleased to see you."

"Why shouldn't she? I got along with everyone down there."

Belinda smiled. "Think back to when you first arrived. Would you have been happy to see me?"

Barbara could feel herself reddening as she recalled those disastrous first days. "I had issues with you, but we worked it out. And Paul helped."

"Paul knew all about my mermaid origins."

Barbara swallowed hard. The new arrival would speak openly about their carefree mermaid days. She would not know about the secret that Barbara was keeping from Graham. A secret that had been necessary in the early days, but one that could derail their future lives together.

Belinda took out her cell phone and started texting frantically. "I'll let Paul know." She squeezed Barbara's hand. "You'll have to tell Graham the minute he arrives in Carden. You can't stall any longer."

Barbara thought of the elaborate preparations that had gone into the weekend's festivities. Graham's daughter was hosting a dinner party to celebrate their engagement, and on Sunday, they would all go on a wine-tasting tour in the Niagara Peninsula. Barbara had planned to wait until they were alone Sunday evening before revealing her mermaid origins.

"Damn!" Belinda threw the phone in her purse, this time, more forcefully. "Paul's going to be delayed in Hamilton. He won't be here until just before dinner." She took several deep breaths and centered herself. "As long as Graham arrives first, we won't have a problem."

Barbara nodded. "And even if he doesn't, I'll take the new girl aside and explain the situation. I can't think of a single mermaid who would not keep my secret."

"I hope you're right. But there's something you're overlooking: She won't be alone."

A mermaid's first few days on Earth were memorable ones. Barbara sighed as she recalled the many stories that had circulated around the Kingdom. It was not unusual for a human male to drape his mermaid love in furs, often mink or ermine, and whisk her away to a lavish honeymoon suite. The first week would be filled with shopping expeditions where thousands of dollars were spent on designer wardrobes and jewelry.

Tears welled in Barbara's eyes as she recalled her own experience. All proclamations of love had been set aside as soon as her human lover had set eyes upon her altered appearance. Alone and practically destitute, Barbara had not been able to board a plane and arrive anywhere in any style. This new ex-mermaid would arrive, smiling and confident, on her man's arm.

"He'll have eyes only for her," Belinda said in a faraway voice. "The relationship is still at the honeymoon stage, so he may not even bother with the rest of us. But there's one question that keeps nagging at me. Why are they coming here?"

"I came here and so did you," Barbara said.

"You didn't have any other option," Belinda said. "As for me, this was Paul's home base until—" She blushed.

"Until you threatened to leave him unless he moved all his business to New York."

"I couldn't see myself spending the rest of my life here." She pointed a finger at Barbara. "You didn't last a year in this . . . this hamlet."

As Barbara drained the last of her coffee, she thought back to the five months she had spent in this small town on the outskirts of Toronto. She had been forced to support herself and build a life as a single woman. While she had found wonderful friends who had helped launch her first career, all that Carden goodwill had evaporated when Barbara made one fatal error of judgment.

Belinda stood. "We need to get back to the house before any of the others. I imagine that's the address—"

A male voice carried through the restaurant. "Look at that black beauty. You don't see too many of those cars around here."

Barbara and Belinda turned toward the picture window. A black BMW had pulled up in front of the restaurant. A small crowd gathered to admire the vehicle.

Belinda laughed. "Only in Carden would a black BMW generate so much interest. It will be the talk of the town for at least a week."

Barbara said nothing but remained seated. She clenched her hands in her lap and looked down. The onions and garlic odor became even more intense. It couldn't be happening. Not again. Not so soon. And not today of all days. It had to be a coincidence.

"What's wrong?" Belinda asked. "If you're worried about how Graham will react, remember we're all here for you. And even if the mermaid spills the beans, we'll help you mop up."

Barbara pointed outside. "The black BMW." Her voice was small and childlike.

"What on Earth does that have to do with anything?"

Before Barbara could explain, a couple appeared at the entrance, a perfectly matched pair. Individually, they could easily turn heads. Together, they were simply phenomenal. The woman was younger by at least a decade, but the man could easily hold his own standing next to her. Barbara focused on the man, painfully reviewing each of his features. The dark-brown, wavy hair without a single strand of gray; beautifully tanned skin that provided the perfect canvas for mesmerizing green eyes with dark eyebrows and long, black eyelashes. The Roman nose and charming cleft on his chin completed the picture-perfect looks that could belong to only one person: Stewart Tobin.

"Arabella," Belinda whispered. "My Arabella."

Barbara's attention switched to the woman standing next to Stewart. Almost as tall, she commanded as much attention, if not more, from the other patrons in the restaurant. Her flawless porcelain skin was framed by long, wavy auburn hair that brushed her shoulders. Her eyes were dark pools, striking in contrast to the pale skin.

Barbara tried to avert her gaze but couldn't. The woman's eyes held her captive as the couple approached. Belinda met them halfway and embraced the woman she had called Arabella. As the two women stood next to each other, there was a collective gasp in the restaurant. While the eyes were different and there was an obvious age difference, the hair and other facial features matched perfectly. There was definitely a relationship, one that Belinda had chosen to publicly acknowledge. As Barbara watched the two women, an intense envy overcame her.

Stewart winked at Barbara. "We are now officially family."

CHAPTER 2

Belinda had eyes only for Arabella while the younger woman coolly appraised every other woman in the restaurant. Satisfied that she was the prettiest, she sighed contentedly. Belinda tore her eyes away and smiled at Barbara. "This is Arabella. Finally, after all these years, we are united."

Arabella nodded toward Barbara. "So, we are sisters, sisters born within seconds of each other."

Stewart laughed. "Arabella, honey, you'll have to change that story. No one's going to believe that you and Barbara are twin sisters. Not by a long shot."

Barbara's cheeks burned. This was definitely payback time. The spurned man was finally getting back at her. He had not forgotten or forgiven the telephone conversation that had ended any hope of a relationship, and he had not appreciated the return of his generous gift—a black BMW.

Hoping to quell the sparks that were starting to fly, Belinda spoke. "We'll continue with the cousin story. It's worked so far. We've told everyone that Barbara and I are first cousins, the daughters of two sisters who were estranged for many years."

Arabella batted her eyelashes. "And what will you say about me?"

"I will tell everyone that you are my daughter from a youthful indiscretion," Belinda said. "I'm sure Paul will go along with it."

Of course, Paul will go along with it. When has he ever not given in or turned his world upside down to please you? While Barbara had also gone along with the cousin story, she still had moments where she would have liked to tell everyone in her circle that Belinda Armstrong was her long-lost mother.

"But first, I need to know your Earth name," Belinda said.

"I've kept my name." Arabella flashed her ring. "And added Tobin to it."

Barbara found her voice. "How were you able to convince Annabella?" When Barbara had left the Kingdom, she had given up any hope of keeping her own mermaid name—Isabella—but losing her name was the least of her many losses. Barbara shuddered as she recalled how savagely Annabella had cut her beautiful auburn hair and then reprogrammed the transformation unit. Annabella's lips had curled into a satisfied smile as the granddaughter she had once loved and adored lost her perfect Bella looks. Shocked into silence, Barbara had watched helplessly as her tail disappeared and a strange, unattractive body emerged.

Arabella laughed, an annoying tinkle. "I told Annabella what I expected, and she gave it to me. She owed me, and she knew it."

Belinda's voice rose. "She certainly did, and I'm glad you stood up to her."

Barbara forced herself to smile. She was the interloper, the third party in all of this. It was a family reunion of mother and daughter—the perfectly preserved mother and daughter.

Stewart nudged Barbara. "It's too bad you didn't stand up to Annabella. If you had, you might still have your youth."

"That was so mean of her," Arabella said. "Aging you like that. How many years did she add?"

As if you didn't know. "Thirty years and she added twenty pounds." *May as well put it all on the table.*

"Which you took off and kept off," Belinda said. "You've done an amazing job of transforming yourself." She squeezed Barbara's hand.

A frown appeared on Arabella's unlined face.

Stewart leaned over and kissed her forehead. "Frowning is not allowed, Bella. I don't want you aging unnecessarily."

Belinda reached forward and put her hand over Arabella's. "He's right. You have absolutely nothing to frown about. You're young and beautiful and have the world at your feet."

Arabella kissed Stewart on the lips and then kissed Belinda on the cheek. "I'm so lucky to have you in my life and . . ." She grabbed Stewart's hand and squealed. "Can we tell them now?"

"Now's not the time. We'll do it later, after dinner." He reluctantly shifted his gaze to Barbara. "Sounds like quite a shindig you've got planned for tonight. When we stopped off at the house, that frazzled young woman was beside herself. Food all over the kitchen. Flowers arriving. Houseguests at the door."

"She wasn't too happy to see us," Arabella said. "I could tell by those eyes of her. Lovely color but so cold."

No hiding or pussyfooting around with Gwen Scott. Barbara thought back to that Christmas dinner when Gwen had barely acknowledged her presence and proceeded to ignore her for the rest of the meal. A Daddy's girl through and through, it had taken almost a year before Gwen spoke directly to her.

"Thank goodness her husband was there," Stewart said. "He knew where to find you, and he invited us to tonight's party." He saluted Barbara with an empty water glass. "I take it congratulations are in order."

Arabella blew her a kiss. "I can hardly wait to meet Graham tonight. My brother-in-law to be."

"That reminds me." Belinda lowered her voice to a whisper. "Barbara would appreciate it if you didn't mention anything about the mermaid world. She hasn't told Graham yet."

"You've got to be kidding," Stewart said.

Arabella's eyes widened. "Stewart knew from the start."

Barbara clenched her teeth. Tonight would be the first time the two men would actually be in the same room, and Barbara wouldn't put it past Stewart to drop a few hints and provoke Graham.

"Barbara's situation is more complicated than yours," Belinda said. "I don't know how much you know—"

Arabella waved her hand and spoke directly to Barbara. "I know all about Adam . . . Anthony . . . What's his name?"

"Andrew Bradley III," Stewart said with a flourish.

"I heard how he dumped you on the shore." Arabella gazed adoringly at Stewart. "I can't even imagine something like that happening to me."

Barbara longed to get out of there, but she wouldn't give Arabella the satisfaction of driving her away. She was also curious about her twin sister who had been banished to the isle of Crete, all because of those dark pools that had frightened their grandmother.

In the Mediterranean Kingdom, there was a definite hierarchy, primarily based upon looks. Auburn-haired with green eyes and porcelain skin, the Bellas were treated like royalty. Next in line were the Annas with varying shades of light brown hair and green eyes. As a Bella, Barbara was allowed only to associate with the Annas, and two of them served as her grandmother's companions. The Ettas were the party girls, blond and pretty with blue eyes, and most likely to be lured away by human males. Close behind were the Inas, not as pretty as the Ettas but still attractive with their trademark blond hair and blue eyes. The most enterprising of the mermaids, Inas were content to stay in the Kingdom, but occasionally one did fall in love with a human. At the base of the pyramid were the Onas, Number Mermaids, and mermen. While their appearance varied, there was a greater probability of dark hair and dark eyes.

As chief elder of the Kingdom, Annabella could not wrap her head around a granddaughter who did meet the exacting Bella standards, so she reacted by banishing the newborn infant to Crete.

"How did you two meet?" Belinda asked.

Arabella and Stewart exchanged glances.

"I'll start the story," Stewart said as he leaned back in his chair. "I was visiting some friends in Crete. One evening, I decided to take a walk by myself. The party had gotten out of hand with alcohol and drugs flowing too freely for my taste. While walking, I saw what looked like a big fish leap out of the water. At first, I thought it was my imagination but the fish kept leaping in and out. I took out my phone and walked quickly toward the shore. But before I could take a picture, the big fish swam to the shore and headed for a large rock."

Arabella squeezed his arm. "Let me finish. It had been a very busy day in the Kingdom, and I was dying to get some time on my own. As soon as I got to the big rock, I felt some pressure on my arm. I turned around and found this beautiful man gazing at me." She spoke directly to Stewart. "That's when I fell in love with you."

Barbara's thoughts traveled back to her own fateful meeting with Andrew. Annabella had been away at the time, dealing with squabbles in Crete. After hearing about the Ettas' elaborate plans to meet men in Annabella's absence, Barbara decided to venture out to shore with two of her Anna friends. While frolicking, the three young mermaids laughed and sang under the darkening Mediterranean sky. A lone man appeared, at first angry to find he was not alone, but he didn't stay angry too long. Eventually, his features softened and he joined in their laughter.

Barbara's heart had fluttered as she stole glances at his features. In the moonlight, he appeared striking with dark, wavy hair and soulful brown eyes. He was the first human male she had ever encountered, and she thought he was beautiful.

He had teased and flirted with all of them, but gradually his attention focused only on Barbara. Their first conversation was firmly embedded in Barbara's memory.

She had boldly asked, "What is your name?"

"Andrew. Andrew Bradley III." He smiled, displaying a perfect set of teeth. "And what is your name?"

"Isabella."

"A beautiful name for a beautiful mermaid."

Their relationship had blossomed while Annabella was away. Barbara listened as Andrew spoke of his newly divorced status and the loneliness that engulfed him. He wanted a companion. He wanted her.

Arabella's annoying giggle brought Barbara back to the present. Stewart had moved closer and taken her into his arms. A deep, soul-searching kiss followed. Belinda motioned to the waiter. "Bring us a bottle of your best champagne. We're celebrating my daughter's marriage to this lovely man."

This lovely man who almost destroyed my life. Had Belinda forgotten all the stunts he pulled and how I had to leave Carden in disgrace? Was she so blinded by this perfect daughter of hers?

"I want to hear the rest," Belinda said.

"I decided to extend my stay," Stewart said. "I met with Arabella every night and by the end of the week, I knew that I wanted her in my life forever."

"I had to go through Aunt Sarabella first." Arabella made a face. "She ignored me, but I persisted, and she finally contacted Annabella."

Belinda frowned. "Was Sarabella unkind to you?"

Barbara wondered about the aunt who had been banished because her lips were not as full as Belinda's. Annabella tolerated imperfections in others but could not accept any flaws within her own family.

Arabella rolled her eyes. "Not really unkind, but she had her hands full with her own brood and constant fighting

with Annabella. As long as Grandmother didn't visit too often, she was happy. My leaving would require a visit from Annabella."

"That old fish is something else," Stewart said. "She didn't scare me, but I knew that I had to keep in her good graces if I wanted Arabella to leave with me."

Annabella neither encouraged nor discouraged mermaids from seeking human companionship. She was aware of the nightly excursions organized by the Ettas and only mildly admonished the mermaids who decided to leave the Kingdom. Before giving her approval, Annabella did a background check and insisted on meeting the man. If the man's finances were not in order, or if she felt he would be abusive in any way, Annabella would not allow the mermaid to leave.

When Barbara had asked permission to leave, Annabella had reacted very differently. Her eyes had blazed as she delivered her scathing remarks. "You are your mother's daughter, through and through. Thoughtless and vain. Inconsiderate. Flighty. Totally useless. I regret having ever loved you."

Belinda rewarded Stewart with a smile. "You were able to negotiate a good package."

Stewart spread his hands wide. "It was all Arabella. She knew exactly what she wanted, and she got it. As you can see, she kept her name and her youthful beauty. She also got that tablet with mermaid support for five years."

"Five years!" Belinda and Barbara spoke in unison.

"I thought I had done well by getting two years," Belinda said. "Paul and I had to fight tooth and nail for that accommodation."

Barbara had given up her tablet the previous week. She and Lisa738 had cried together as they waved goodbye. From the start, the Numbers Mermaid had given Barbara her unconditional support. Without Lisa738, Barbara could never have secured employment or written a bestselling book; and when the Cardeners took distance, Lisa738 had helped Barbara pick up the shattered shards of her well-constructed human life and reinvent herself once more. Belinda and Paul had urged her to renegotiate with Annabella, but Barbara refused to have anything further to do with her grandmother.

"What I would give to get a prototype of that tablet." Stewart's eyes gleamed. "And the patent, of course. I would be set for life."

As if you aren't already. How much more money do you need to be "set" for life? Barbara's lips tightened as she recalled the loaded Ferrari and all the other accoutrements of wealth she had observed during that weekend in Chicago.

"That's not possible," Belinda gasped. "You mustn't even think of it."

Stewart shook his finger playfully at her. "Now, don't tell me that Paul Armstrong hasn't considered it." He snapped his fingers. "Imagine, having access to those magical buttons loaded with Specialist Skills. Pick one and presto, you can golf like Tiger Woods or paint like Picasso."

Barbara wondered what Skills Arabella had selected but did not want to engage her sister in conversation. Belinda was frowning and trying to figure out a way of changing the topic.

Stewart persisted. "We've got five years. I'll charm the Numbers Mermaid into revealing the secrets behind that technology."

Arabella's mouth curved into a wicked smile as her gaze shifted to Barbara. "It's too bad you didn't get to keep your tablet beyond a year. But if it's any consolation, I got Lisa738 as my Numbers Mermaid."

"You got Lisa738," Barbara repeated as tears flowed freely down her cheeks. *This was the final blow*. Barbara grabbed her purse, donned her sunglasses, and headed outdoors.

As Barbara approached her car, she felt light pressure on her arm. Belinda had caught up with her. While her mother's eyes were hidden behind dark glasses, her lips trembled. "I know this is hard, Barbara. But in spite of outward appearances, it's not that easy for Arabella either. She hasn't been on Earth that long."

"Long enough to get married and get support from Lisa738."

"You chose not to keep her," Belinda said. "You didn't want another confrontation with Annabella."

"So, you agree that Arabella somehow manipulated Annabella into giving her Lisa738?"

"You've made Arabella into a villain. Unjustly so, I might add. It must be difficult to come face to face with a younger version of yourself and imagine what could have been." Belinda paused. "Keep in mind that, if Annabella had not taken away your youth, you would never have met Graham or connected with me. You would not have written that bestselling book and created such a wonderful life for yourself. No one, absolutely no one, can take that away from you."

Both women were crying freely as they embraced.

"I know it's hard to watch me welcome Arabella and acknowledge her as my daughter. I longed to do that with you, but the circumstances just didn't allow it."

They had rehashed the situation many times and always reached the same conclusion. There was no way that forty-five-year-old Belinda Armstrong could acknowledge a fifty-four-year-old daughter.

CHAPTER 3

Barbara did not remove her sunglasses until she reached the safety of her room. Thankfully, there were no other cars in the driveway, and Gwen was otherwise occupied in the kitchen. Barbara could not have handled conversations with any of them, not even Graham. And that was one conversation she could not put off much longer.

How would he respond? Would he slowly nod and wait for her to finish speaking? Or would he demand to know why she had kept him in the dark for so long? Barbara could imagine either scenario. While her relationship with Graham had evolved, there were still moments where he distanced himself.

It was all about trust.

Barbara had failed a major test when she had slept with Stewart and kept both men dangling. The main issue was that Graham had no idea he was being dangled until that fateful day when the black BMW arrived, in full view of everyone at her workplace and anyone who happened to be walking by. Barbara shuddered at the memory of Graham's angry eyes as he confronted her and dismissed her feeble attempts to provide an explanation.

There was nothing she could do until Graham arrived. Her eyes traveled to the standard alarm clock on the night table. Barely two o'clock. There was still time. Slipping out of her shoes and stockings, Barbara decided not to bother with the rest of her clothes. She threw herself on the bed and closed her eyes.

"Wake up, Barbara! Wake up!"

Barbara woke up to a familiar voice from her mermaid past.

Barbara sat up and looked directly into the emerald-green eyes of Annabella who was floating above the night table. "Grandmother! What are you doing here?"

"Did you really think I would abandon you?"

Barbara threw up her hands. "You haven't helped at all."

"How can I help if you refuse to have any contact with me?" Annabella sighed. "I would have given you an extension with the tablet. All you had to do was ask."

"So, you gave Lisa738 to Arabella. Is that your way of getting back at me?"

Annabella exhaled sharply. "The Kingdom was at stake."

Barbara rolled her eyes. "While I love Lisa738 dearly, I can't see her as a power player in the running of the Mediterranean Kingdom."

"It was one of the demands I had to meet to ensure peace. Sarabella decided to play hardball and Arabella joined in the game."

"How is Sarabella involved?"

"I felt guilty after I banished Sarabella to Crete and tried to make it up to her by grooming her as chief elder of the island. She appeared compliant, but when she reached adulthood, she changed her tune. There have been over two decades of disharmony." Annabella's shoulders drooped and her mouth tightened.

While she wanted to know more about Arabella's involvement, Barbara was also curious about her aunt. Barbara had been aware of problems on the island of Crete, but she hadn't known that her aunt was the main instigator. It wasn't until her chance meeting with Belinda on Earth that Barbara learned about Sarabella's existence.

"What type of disharmony?"

"Mainly power grabbing," Annabella replied. "Not consulting me about major decisions, and she doesn't treat those mermen right. They are punished whenever they complain or take too long to complete their tasks. I always feared some kind of uprising. Worse is that, somehow, Arabella wormed her way into Sarabella's graces, and the two of them have been wreaking havoc with the computer system."

Barbara had always marveled at the sight of enormous mainframe computers that took up significant space in the Kingdom. And she had wondered why armies of mermen continually sprayed the computers, stopping only when the next shift arrived. During her first month on Earth, she had deduced the answer. That special coating meticulously applied throughout the day prevented oceans of water from damaging the computers.

Annabella and the other elders had their own tablets, but only the Numbers mermaids had access to the information stored in the data banks. Whenever Barbara had expressed interest in the computer systems, Annabella had smiled and informed her there was plenty of time to learn all of that later.

During her conversations with Lisa738, Barbara had been surprised to discover that the Kingdom's technology was at least two generations ahead of the Earth's. Detailed records of all mermaids, mermen, and ex-mermaids touched on all aspects of their lives. Everything from a mild headache to an indiscretion was recorded.

"What have they done?" Barbara asked.

"They hacked into the system and accessed all our files. They even got into the tablets." Annabella paused. "Arabella knows every single detail about your life here on Earth."

Barbara gave a bitter laugh. "And you still gave her Lisa738."

"While I was dealing with the fallout from the hacking, Arabella met Stewart. I was more than willing to let her go, and Sarabella didn't really care one way or another. But

Arabella suddenly became difficult. She refused to reveal a critical password unless she got her way, so we had to negotiate."

"You mean, give in to all her demands."

"At the time, they didn't seem excessive."

"Maybe not to you."

Annabella leaned over and whispered, "Now that you know the story, you can arm yourself."

"'Arm myself,'" Barbara repeated. "Am I to do battle with Arabella?"

"Be careful." Annabella blew her a kiss and faded away.

"What do you mean?" Barbara shouted, "Come back here!"

There was a knock at the door. "Barbara, are you all right? It's me, Gillian."

Barbara glanced down at her rumpled clothes and caught a glimpse of bed hair in the mirror. If it were anyone else, she would tell him or her to go away. But Gillian, knew all her secrets.

Geographically, they were miles apart but regular phone calls to Chicago had staved off Barbara's loneliness and given her the confidence to set goals and achieve them. With Gillian's advice, Barbara had been able to shed the extra pounds and reinvent herself as a career counselor, motivational speaker, and author; all in less than a year and, for most of the time, without a man on her arm.

Gillian poked her head around the door. Her blond hair was beautifully styled and a string of pearls set off her lightly tanned skin. The formfitting black dress and high heels made her seem even leaner and taller. She was an Etta, through and through. Her eyes widened in alarm as she took in Barbara's dishevelled appearance. "Why haven't you changed? Everyone's downstairs."

"Isn't it fashionable to be late?" Barbara asked.

Gillian walked over and hugged her. "This has nothing to do with being fashionable. You're upset, and I know why."

"You've met her."

"Oh, yes. She's holding court downstairs and if you don't pull yourself together, she'll take over your engagement party."

Barbara sucked in a breath. "Has Graham arrived?"

"He's downstairs waiting. If it's any consolation, he's amused by the beautiful and effervescent Arabella. And so is Andrew, I may add." Gillian smiled confidently, secure in the knowledge that her man would not be tempted. "Now, let's get moving here. Do something with that hair, and I'll help you with your makeup."

Barbara went into the adjoining bathroom, splashed her face with cold water, and dabbed it dry. As the curling iron heated up, she examined her features in the mirror. Thankfully, she had retained the striking green eyes and flawless skin of her mermaid days. The red-gold wavy tresses were gone, but she had a good handle on her straight butterscotch colored hair. Within minutes, she tamed her hair into a sleek pageboy.

Back in the bedroom, Gillian worked her makeup magic. She stood back and admired her handiwork. "Simply beautiful. You'll wow them all." She pointed to the closet. "What dress are you wearing?"

Barbara walked over and took out a sleek, emerald-green sheath. She stepped into the dress and had Gillian zip her up.

Both women turned toward the mirror and nodded in satisfaction.

Gillian tapped her foot impatiently. "Now, let's go."

"What is she wearing?"

"She's wearing a lacy white micro-mini that shows off those endless legs and doesn't leave much to the imagination." Gillian gripped Barbara's shoulders. "She'll be playing games all night, but that's to be expected of a newly arrived mermaid, fresh and confident in her looks and her man."

"I never had that," Barbara said sadly.

"But you have so much more, and you got it on your terms. Don't let that pretty little twenty-four-year-old mess with your mind."

CHAPTER 4

As Barbara and Gillian descended, they could hear the whistles. Graham rushed to the staircase and enveloped Barbara in a long passionate kiss. Everyone clapped and cheered. When they came up for air, Belinda and Paul were at Barbara's side. Belinda hugged her, and Paul whispered, "You're beautiful!"

Barbara's eyes traveled back to Graham. In his dark-blue suit, he was more handsome than ever and for several moments, all she could do was smile contentedly at him. Thoughts of Arabella and Stewart faded as she gazed directly into lively hazel eyes that held so much love and kindness. If only she could have a few minutes to explain everything. *You had seven months to tell him everything.* The intrusive thought froze the smile on her face. She couldn't let anyone, especially Graham, think that anything could possibly be wrong. She reluctantly tore away her gaze and took in the other guests.

Gwen nodded in her direction. The smile was still forced, but they had made considerable progress in their relationship. The devoted Daddy's girl had finally accepted that Barbara was part of Graham's life, and she had even volunteered to host this engagement dinner. Her husband, Sammy, winked and gave Barbara a thumbs-up. From the start, the young man had been one of her greatest fans, and Barbara suspected he was responsible for Gwen's change of heart.

Andrew blew her a kiss. Barbara smiled back. Last year, about this time, she was cursing him for abandoning her, but all had been forgiven. When they had met several months after that traumatic event, Andrew had begged for Barbara's forgiveness. Barbara found herself more than willing to forgive him, especially after learning he had returned to the beach, only to find her gone. She had no qualms about his blossoming relationship with Gillian. Her first love had moved on, and so had she.

Barbara had a hard time figuring out Stewart's reaction. She had only spent two days with him, but that fling has set off a series of events with disastrous consequences. It would be a while, if ever, before Barbara could feel comfortable and confident in Stewart's presence. There was tightness in his jaw, but she wasn't close enough to see his eyes, those expressive green eyes that matched hers and were so transparent. If she had been standing closer, she could have figured out whether he still had some feelings for her, or if he was plotting his revenge.

Arabella was smirking. There was no other way to describe the arrogance that marred her features. Barbara took in the whole picture, from the carelessly tossed auburn tresses to the strappy nude-colored sandals. The white micro-mini hugged every curve, leaving absolutely nothing to the imagination. Her only accessories were the diamonds that flashed at her ears and on her finger. The look was a nonchalant one that said, *I don't have to try too hard.*

Paul spoke first. "I don't know about any of you, but after all this feasting on beautiful women, I'm hungry and ready to eat the wonderful dinner that my granddaughter has prepared."

Everyone laughed and headed toward the dining room. Barbara winced as she made her way there. She had promised Gwen that she would help, and instead, she had slept through the entire afternoon. However, everything was beautifully in place. If organized and meticulous Gwen had been put out by her lack of help and the extra two guests, she wasn't showing it. She was actually laughing in response to one of Stewart's comments. Barbara made a mental note to take Gwen aside and thank her for hosting the party.

Stewart pointed to the table and pulled Arabella toward him. "My beautiful and accomplished wife created that centerpiece out of twigs and whatever she could find lying around."

Sammy smiled enthusiastically at Arabella. "Gwen and I really appreciate you pitching in like that."

"Arabella's a real trouper," Belinda said. "As soon as she arrived, she figured out what had to be done and did it." She smiled ruefully. "I don't think I would have been traipsing outside if I had been all dressed up."

Arabella accepted these compliments with that annoying tinkle of a laugh.

As they took their places, Barbara breathed a sigh of relief. Either Belinda or Gillian must have created the seating plan. Flanked by Graham and Paul and across from Gillian, Barbara felt comfortable and at ease. She was far enough away from Arabella who was basking in the male attention from Stewart and Sammy and the motherly love emanating from Belinda. Gwen frowned at her husband's fawning and tried to catch his eye, but he didn't seem to notice.

Paul stood and took charge. "Thank you all for coming. I want to start by thanking Gwen for organizing this party in honor of Barbara and Graham. This house has been in our family for over a hundred years, and I'm glad to see it passed down to the next generation." He raised his wineglass. "Let us raise our glasses to my son and his beautiful fiancée. May you experience a lifetime of joy and happiness, beyond your wildest dreams. Barbara and Graham."

Everyone stood and toasted the couple.

The meal was outstanding. Barbara had expected vegetarian fare and was pleasantly surprised to find beef bourguignon on the menu, perfectly flavored and accompanied by steamed rice, sautéed green beans and Gwen's signature beet and arugula salad. They ended the meal with Graham's favorite dessert, amaretto cheesecake.

Throughout the meal, Barbara cringed whenever she heard Arabella's laugh. Her nose started tickling again as she breathed in what could only be described as burnt coffee beans, definitely not a pleasant smell. She wondered what more could possibly happen.

As the meal progressed, the laugh became shriller.

"Someone's getting sauced," Graham muttered.

Barbara watched as Stewart continued to pour generous amounts of wine into Arabella's glass. Why was he doing that? Didn't he realize that Arabella was still getting used to her new human body and couldn't really judge how much alcohol was enough? She closed her eyes and recalled her own disastrous experience with too much wine.

On the day that Graham and everyone else in Carden learned of her affair with Stewart Tobin, Barbara had consumed half a bottle of pinot grigio. Barely able to speak or even stand, she had watched helplessly as Graham had broken off their relationship. Afterward, she had knocked the wine bottle off the coffee table, staining the pale-gray carpet and activating the tablet. When Lisa738 appeared, she burst into tears and faded away into the screen. It had not been pleasant and Barbara had no desire to see her newly found sister in a similar state.

"I think she's had enough," Paul said.

Everyone stopped speaking and followed Paul's gaze. Stewart shrugged and put the bottle down. Arabella hiccupped loudly. An awkward silence followed. Arabella stood up, groggy but determined. She lifted her almost-empty glass toward Barbara and Graham. "It's my turn to toast."

"We've already had a toast." Belinda's eyes widened in alarm as she made eye contact with Stewart, imploring him to intervene.

Before anyone could move, Arabella pointed her glass toward Barbara. A few drops spilled and stained the white damask tablecloth. "And here's to you, dear mermaid sister. Separated at birth, we're finally together again. And we'll always be together with the mother we never knew and the men who love us." She made eye contact with Stewart. "Can I tell them now?"

Paul appeared at her side. "I think you've told them enough. Let's get you outside." He glared at Stewart as he firmly took Arabella's arm.

Gwen frowned at Barbara. "I thought you and Belinda were cousins. Why is she saying that Belinda is her mother and yours as well?"

Graham winked at Gwen. "She's drunk, honey. And I don't think she knows what she's saying. None of it makes any sense."

Barbara found herself speechless. The unthinkable had happened, and now she must decide how to proceed. In the back of her mind, she knew one option that was readily available to her. Dismiss Arabella's rant and continue keeping her mermaid past a secret. Belinda and Paul would honor her wishes, and so would Gillian and Andrew. Stewart, though, was another story. When Barbara reluctantly made eye contact with Stewart, she immediately recognized that glint of steel in his eyes.

"It's time to tell him the truth," Stewart said. "You've kept him in the dark long enough."

"I think it's time for you to leave," Graham said quietly. "You and your wife have upset us enough for one evening."

Barbara's heart pounded wildly and her throat constricted. She forced herself to stand. Her eyes swam with tears, and she blinked hard, trying to stop them from overflowing. "I'm so sorry, Graham. This wasn't how I planned to tell you." She blocked out everyone else in the room and focused only on Graham, both fearing and anticipating his reaction to the news that could potentially derail their relationship.

"When I arrived in Carden last fall, everyone believed my story about leaving a disastrous marriage and relocating to Canada, but none of it was true. I didn't leave a philandering husband in Arizona, and I'm not really Barbara Davies. I am Isabella of the Mediterranean tribe. Gillian, Belinda, and Arabella are also of that tribe." She managed a smile. "In spite of her inebriated state, Arabella is correct. Belinda is our mother. You see, Arabella and I are twins, Bella twins. When we were born, our grandmother took one look at Arabella's dark eyes and shuddered. Grandmother banished Arabella to Crete. Shortly after our birth, Belinda decided to leave the Kingdom with Paul. She was transformed into human form and was forced to leave both of us behind. We were too young to undergo the transformation process."

Barbara felt light pressure on her arm and caught a glimpse of Belinda's eyes filling with tears. Barbara continued. "With Belinda out of the picture, Grandmother focused on me and raised me to be an elder of the Kingdom. All that changed when I met Andrew. I fell madly in love and begged Grandmother to let me go. She was displeased and, in a fit of rage, transformed me into an overweight, middle-aged woman."

Andrew's head was bowed, and Gillian was holding on to his arm. Barbara continued, "I don't blame Andrew for leaving me. I found out later that he had returned, but I was long gone. Grandmother whisked me across the ocean to Carden. And that's where my human life really began."

Barbara could see the disbelief and confusion that simmered in Graham's eyes. "So many times I wanted to sit down and tell you everything, but I could never find the words. I fully intended to tell you everything tomorrow evening and give you the option of leaving, if it was too much for you."

She wiped away the tears from her eyes and focused on Stewart. "I don't know whether or not you planned this early disclosure. I want to tell you that you have succeeded in ruining what should have been the happiest day of my life. I guess we're even now."

Barbara ran up the stairs to her room.

CHAPTER 5

Barbara awoke to a shaft of sunlight on her face. Jumbled thoughts raced through her mind as she searched for a clock. *What time is it and why is the sun so bright?* It was her first night sleeping at the house that she would always think of as belonging to Graham's dead wife, and now their cool, distant daughter owned it. Thoughts of Gwen brought her to a standstill. Barbara had been in a hurry to leave the dining room, and she hadn't even bothered to check Gwen's reaction to the news. With a sinking heart, she also realized that she had not properly thanked her for hosting the engagement party.

Barbara finally located the clock and noticed it was after ten. Why had she slept so long? She thought back to the previous evening's events. After her hasty departure, she had heard several doors slam and loud voices below. Thankfully, she couldn't make out what anyone was saying.

She stretched into a yawn and made her way into the adjoining bathroom. When she glanced in the mirror, she groaned. Her eyes were still puffy, and her skin had a gray cast. It would take a while to put her game face on.

Half an hour later, she went downstairs. The house was eerily quiet, but the aroma of freshly percolated coffee and bacon greeted her. Someone had prepared breakfast. When she reached the dining room, Paul was sitting there reading his paper. He smiled warmly at her. "I took the liberty of making breakfast for you."

Barbara raised her eyebrows. "I didn't know you could cook."

Paul winked. "Had to learn when I was between wives. It's been a while, but I don't think I've lost my touch with omelettes."

Barbara sat down and stared at the beautiful place setting that could have appeared in one of Martha Stewart's cookbooks. She managed a smile and started to speak but stopped when Paul held up his hand.

"Go on and eat before it gets cold," Paul said. "We'll talk after." He went back to reading his newspaper.

As Barbara ate, her eyes traveled around the room. All evidence of last night's dinner had been removed. Someone had stayed up late last night or gotten up early to clean, and it was probably Gwen.

"She's not here," Paul said. "She and Sammy went on the wine-tasting tour."

Barbara had forgotten all about the tour. Graham had meticulously planned every detail, delighted about sharing one of his favorite pastimes with Barbara and the others. To make the experience even more memorable, he had made reservations for eight on the Via Rail Fiesta tour. A stretch limo would take them to the Oakville station and pick them up later in the day, leaving them free to indulge in some of the best wines in the region. The day would be filled with visits to four different wineries, wine tasting, shopping, and a gourmet lunch. Barbara wrung her hands. "Did anyone else go?"

Paul put down the paper. "No one else was really in the mood. The only reason Gwen went is because, well, she . . ."

"She didn't want to see me this morning," Barbara said. "Not to worry. I'll be gone as soon as I finish breakfast. What about the others?"

"After your announcement, the evening quickly went downhill. Gillian and Andrew went back to the Carden Inn. Arabella never did come back inside. Stewart also made a quick exit. Your mother and I stayed for a while, but it was clear that Gwen wanted us to leave. She flew into a rage and said a few things that I'm sure she regrets this morning."

"And Graham?" Barbara's heart thundered in her chest.

"He said nothing, absolutely nothing. He got into his car and drove back to Cobourg. He left a message with Gwen." Paul handed Barbara a small piece of notepaper.

Accepted a teaching position in Vermont.

"For how long?" Barbara whispered.

"Probably until Christmas," Paul said. "But it could be longer. He might also have agreed to teach during the winter term. It takes a while for Graham to let go of grudges." His features darkened as he lowered his gaze.

While she had heard some of the details from Belinda, Barbara had only a vague picture of just how desolate Paul must have been during those dark years. Paul had met Wife #2 during Graham's first week in kindergarten. A month later, Paul asked for a divorce. Graham's mother had stoically accepted her husband's decision, but her son was another matter. He threw tantrums whenever he saw Paul and refused to attend school. After Christmas, Graham's mother decided to move away and give Graham a fresh start in Barrie. Paul continued to visit and support his first family, but he could never chat, throw a ball, or engage in any activity with Graham. The day after his twenty-first birthday, Graham assumed his mother's maiden name.

Barbara leaned over and squeezed his hand. "How long did he stay away?"

Paul's eyes glistened with tears. "On the day of his eighteenth birthday, he stopped taking my calls and refused to visit. That went on for nine years. If it weren't for that kind and generous woman he married, we would never have reconciled." He shuddered. "I would never have met my grandchildren or you."

"Nine years! I don't think I can wait that long."

Paul shook his head. "If he was able to forgive your affair with Stewart, I think he can move past this. One thing I know for sure. He won't stay in Vermont during Christmas. The college closes down for the holiday and everyone disperses."

"Two months without Graham." Barbara's thoughts raced back to their quarrel earlier in the year. Somehow, she had managed to survive without seeing him for three months, but it had not been easy. If it hadn't been for Lisa738, she would never have survived those first two weeks.

"I shouldn't have listened to Belinda," Paul muttered.

"Excuse me?"

Paul sighed. "I wanted to tell my children about Belinda's mermaid origins long ago, but your mother was afraid everyone would turn on her. She struggled with insecurity for several years and was very protective of her past." He cleared his throat. "My daughters would have been intrigued and Graham, well Graham, might not have cared one way or another, but he would have known about your mermaid origins from the start."

Belinda. Insecure? An incongruous thought, one that Barbara would never have entertained, but Paul appeared very sincere and troubled.

"Keep busy," Paul said. "Book as many speaking engagements as you can and get out of Cobourg on the weekends. Plan outings with your Toronto friends."

Barbara thought ahead to the weeks that loomed before her. She was working full-time and could easily book each day of the week and keep herself so busy that she didn't have time to think. During the evenings and weekends, she could work on the first draft of her next book.

"How much do your colleagues know about your personal life?" Paul asked.

"They know I see Graham regularly, and they've met you and Belinda." Barbara managed a smile. "I didn't tell anyone about the engagement party." She hadn't even worn her engagement ring to work. Had she anticipated this turn of events? Or had she manifested it with her ambivalence and fear?

"Good," Paul said. "You won't have to make any announcements."

"No one will think it odd that Graham is spending two months in Vermont. They all know about his teaching stints there."

"And that's what this is," Paul said. "'A teaching stint' in Vermont."

Barbara's spirits perked up as she mentally started scheduling weekend activities in Toronto. One call to Nico and Mario and she'd be set for two months. She had a standing invitation to join the gay couple for any weekend activity, and she could always stay in Elaine's guest bedroom. Her Toronto friends conveniently lived in the same condo building.

Paul cleared his throat. "And now we need to discuss Arabella."

Barbara swallowed against the hard lump that was forming in her throat. "There's nothing to discuss. I'll be in Cobourg. She'll be in Chicago. Our paths will not cross."

"She's your twin sister. You can't dismiss her and hope she'll stay away."

"I don't . . . trust her."

"You just met her yesterday. How can you form a judgment so quickly?"

Barbara shifted uncomfortably in her chair. "While I don't condone Annabella's behavior, I can see how she would have been put out by Arabella's eyes. They're not natural. And she has that annoying laugh—"

"Women!" Paul exclaimed. "You would think after three wives I would have finally figured out the inner workings of the female mind."

Barbara smiled stiffly. "It's more than that, Paul. Her behavior. Her demeanor. She's so self-absorbed."

"She's twenty-four years old."

"And your point is?"

"That's how twenty-four-year-old women, especially drop-dead gorgeous ones, behave." Paul threw his head back and laughed wholeheartedly. "Belinda was the same. She was only a year older than Arabella when she arrived here, and let me tell you that woman was hell on heels. I had to buy her four fur coats so she could get through a Carden winter in style, and I had to move my entire operations to New York. She threatened to leave me if we didn't get out of Carden."

Barbara couldn't even imagine making such demands of Paul Armstrong. At seventy-seven, he still attracted female attention when he walked into a room. A thick, well-maintained mane of white hair framed his expressive hazel eyes and tanned skin. Impeccably groomed, even when dressed casually in jeans and sweats. As a much younger man, he would have had his pick of women. Yet, he had chosen and stayed with a demanding woman who thought nothing of uprooting his entire life.

"It's too bad you never had the human youth that was rightfully yours." He paused. "That's the problem here. Whenever you meet up with Arabella, you see what could have been, and that must be hard."

"I would never, never have behaved like that," Barbara said. "Dressing that indecently and expecting all the conversation to center around her. She actually pouted when anyone complimented me or the other women in the room." Barbara paused. "Narcissist through and through."

Paul winked. "And so is Belinda. It does run in families, you know."

Barbara's eyes widened. "Do you think I'm narcissistic?"

Paul laughed. "Sweetheart, you're the farthest thing

from a narcissist." He assumed a more serious tone. "Back to Arabella. Like it or not, she's in your life, and you will be seeing more of her."

Barbara wrapped her fingers protectively around her throat. "To see more of her, I'd have to fly out to Chicago or invite her to my home."

"You missed the big announcement last night," Paul said. "Stewart bought the old Melanson home on the outskirts of Carden."

Barbara groaned. "So, they'll be spending their summers here. That's eight months away and a lot can happen."

"Not quite. She persuaded Stewart to leave Chicago and run his business from here."

"You can't be serious!" Barbara's eyes widened. "Stewart Tobin is giving up Chicago for Carden?"

"He's giving up Chicago for Arabella," Paul said. "You know as well as anyone he runs most of his business online, so this is not a hardship."

Barbara thought back to that whirlwind weekend in Chicago. Stewart had wined and dined her and then seduced her in a luxury suite at the Omni Hotel. Chicago was Stewart's town and everywhere he went, people fawned over him. His social calendar was filled months in advance. How on Earth would he survive small-town life?

Paul smiled as he watched the changing expressions on her face. "He's besotted with her, but Belinda thinks he may still have some feelings for you."

"Feelings of revenge, maybe."

"Perhaps," Paul said. "I don't imagine Stewart took too kindly to being dumped."

"The revenge of a scorned man," Barbara said. "Is that what I'm in for?"

"You're only in for what you choose."

"I choose not to have any contact with Arabella and Stewart."

Paul sighed wearily. "That means we won't be seeing much of you, either."

"What do you mean?"

"Belinda is choosing to have Arabella in her life. She plans to spend holidays and as much time as her schedule permits in Ontario."

"She's choosing Arabella over me." Barbara's voice rose as she spoke.

"Arabella is also her daughter. One that was snatched away from her and banished to Crete." Paul glanced at his watch. "I've got to get back to the Carden Inn. Belinda has planned a goodbye brunch for Arabella and Stewart. Gillian and Andrew are also joining us." He raised his eyebrows. "She asked me to invite you."

CHAPTER 6

Barbara arrived in Cobourg shortly after two in the afternoon. There had been an accident on the highway, and she was delayed for over an hour. While that may have stressed her during the work week, on this particular Sunday, Barbara didn't mind the longer commute. She used the time to jot down notes and outline two seminars in her new *Second Acts* series.

Three months had passed since the successful launch of *It's Your Time*, and since then, she had been inundated with speaking requests and suggestions that she write another book focusing on the career and relationship challenges faced by Boomer women hoping to reinvent themselves. Initially overwhelmed by the response, she had been unable to even write a word, but Graham had calmly reassured her. He had even created beautiful butterfly designs for her press releases and PowerPoint presentations.

As soon as she entered the house, she hung up her jacket, made herself a smoothie, and headed toward the den. Working steadily, she wrote up both seminars and prepared a PowerPoint presentation. Her growling stomach forced her to finally leave her laptop.

Glancing at the clock, she was surprised to learn that it was past seven in the evening. She toyed with the idea of ordering a pizza, but her self-discipline overruled that impulse. Since Friday evening, she had eaten twice in restaurants and feasted on Gwen's elaborate dinner and Paul's calorie-laden breakfast.

She gathered all the greens in the fridge, opened a can of tuna and quickly assembled a salad. While munching on her salad, she thought of the week ahead. Last night's debacle still occupied center stage, but she was starting to see one positive emerging. Without Graham around, she could work undistracted and even get started on a proposal for her next book.

After dinner, she sat on her favorite chair, cell phone in hand. She took several deep breaths and dialed Graham's number. The phone rang several times and finally the machine picked up. Tempted to hang up and try again later, Barbara forced herself to leave a message: "I'm so-so sorry, Graham. I know that I should have, um, well, I couldn't. I was just so afraid. I'm . . ." She broke off the connection and sat quietly with her phone in hand.

Within minutes, the telephone rang. *Was he ready to talk?* And maybe, just maybe, forgive her one more time. Without glancing at caller ID, she picked up the receiver.

"How are you doing?" Gillian's low, husky voice was filled with concern.

"I've been better." Tears sprung into Barbara's eyes. "I just called and left a message for Graham."

"I would have called sooner, but we had unexpected guests, so I had to wait until they left." Gillian paused. "Andrew went to the drugstore."

When Barbara and Gillian were unattached, they would spend hours on the phone rehashing events, but their significant others did not approve of gossiping, so their conversations had to take place when the men were not around. While Graham was temporarily, or maybe even permanently, out of the picture, Andrew was still part of Gillian's life and the younger woman had no intention of jeopardizing that relationship. This conversation, like many before it, would end as soon as Andrew's car pulled up in the driveway.

"I'll be quick with the details," Gillian said. "When Belinda invited us for brunch, I ignored the horrified expression on Andrew's face and accepted the invitation. All morning, I had to put up with his rant about how he wanted to strangle Arabella and Stewart. Not that I blame him. I felt the same way, but my curiosity about Sister Dearest won out."

In spite of herself, Barbara laughed.

Gillian continued. "Arabella was late, fashionably so. She was wearing a purple micro-mini that hugged every curve and matching purple stilettos. Where on Earth does she find these clothes? I can't imagine Stewart advising her."

Barbara had wondered the same thing. While Stewart loved his women, he dressed tastefully and expected his companions to follow suit. The clothes were all Arabella. Of that Barbara was certain.

"She created quite the stir in the restaurant," Gillian said. "As she sauntered across the room, appearing lost and confused, she managed to attract everyone's attention. I felt for the two older gentlemen who dropped plates while moving through the buffet line. One of them received a loud tongue-lashing from his wife. The other one started hyperventilating."

How could anyone get lost and confused in the Carden Inn? At most, the restaurant seated sixty people. In late-October, they would be lucky to get twenty patrons for Sunday brunch.

"Belinda was waving madly but, for some reason, Arabella chose not to see her. Stewart finally got up and accompanied her to our table. Belinda had decided on á la carte dining, so Arabella did not have to get up again."

Barbara was so glad she had refused Belinda's invitation. She was grateful for the lovely breakfast Paul had prepared for her, but found it hard to believe that he had sat through all that drama. As had Andrew.

Gillian continued, "Arabella dominated the conversation. She complained about everything from the lumpy bed to a troublesome maid who woke her up to her Numbers Mermaid."

Barbara gasped. "How could she think of complaining about Lisa738?"

"You wouldn't believe the laundry list of complaints," Gillian said. "But her main issue is that Lisa738 never makes eye contact and speaks only in monosyllables. Arabella can never have a proper conversation with her."

While Barbara felt for Lisa738's five-year term with her sister, she was happy to hear that it would not be easy sailing for Arabella. How Barbara wished she could have had one more conversation with Lisa738.

". . . kept harping on the eye contact," Gillian said as Barbara turned her attention back to the conversation. "I found it odd until I remembered her story. She was banished because of those eyes, and from what I know of Crete, those mermaids and mermen would have made her life hell."

Barbara thought back to the previous evening. While she had tried to avoid making direct eye contact with Arabella, she was fascinated by those dark pools. Absolutely no light or change of color. Barbara wondered if that intense darkness was always there and how Stewart dealt with it, especially during their lovemaking.

"Barbara . . . Barbara, are you still there?" Gillian raised her voice.

"Sorry, I was daydreaming," Barbara said. "Anything else to report?"

"Right before dessert, Andrew got up and announced we had to leave. He had had enough. I could tell by the way he was clenching his teeth. And of course, I heard about it later."

"Thank you, Gillian. I know it wasn't easy—"

"Not to worry. I can deal with Andrew. I wanted to keep you posted, and I knew that neither Belinda nor Paul would be able to give you an unbiased account."

"Paul made me breakfast," Barbara said. "And he listened to my rant about Arabella."

"Graham will call. I'm sure of it."

"He left a note with Gwen," Barbra said, her eyes refilling with tears. She felt suddenly overwhelmed by sadness and regret coming from infinite directions.

"And?"

"He's teaching in Vermont." Sobs wracked her chest and her throat closed up.

"He'll be back for Christmas," Gillian said encouragingly as she lowered her voice. "Andrew's pulling up in the driveway. I just want to leave you with some advice. Keep your distance but don't cut off your nose to spite your face. That is, don't stop seeing your mother just so you can avoid seeing your sister. If you do, you will play right into that little witch's hands." Gillian hung up abruptly.

Barbara would have loved to continue the conversation, but it didn't look like they could have another chat for a while. Gillian and Andrew were flying out to Singapore later in the week and they would be gone for several months.

CHAPTER 7

Barbara barely slept. She got out of bed at five and was on the road by six-fifteen. She was the first one to arrive at the Eagle Vision office. Once inside, she made her way to her office. It had been two months since she had left the west end branch, and she still hadn't put her personal touches on the room.

While the desk was clear of clutter and boxes of files were piled neatly in a corner, the room lacked clear definition and color. Like all the other offices at Eagle Vision, it existed only in shades of beige and gray. The Sharon Clarke Decorating Scheme, the others liked to joke. Their budget-conscious boss simply went online and ordered furniture from IKEA. When anyone complained, she suggested they buy their own accessories if they wanted more pizzazz.

To be fair, Barbara only spent four days a month in the office. The rest of the time, she was on the road covering East Toronto and beyond. Barbara didn't plan on cutting back her seminars, but she could come in on Saturdays and Sundays to decorate the office.

Working at a brisk pace, Barbara was able to sort through most of the files. At nine-thirty, she got on the phone and started booking seminars for December and January. Between the incoming and outgoing calls, Barbara was busy until noon. When her stomach announced the lunch hour, she reached for a Vega Bar. She leaned back in her chair, satisfied with the morning's accomplishments.

"Took you long enough to come up for air. This is the third time I've come by to say hello."

Sharon Clarke was never one to mince words. And the veiled criticism in her comments did not go unnoticed. In the past, whenever Barbara had visited the office, she had stopped to chat with Sharon. It was a courtesy that she had not extended today.

"I'm sorry, Sharon. I got here early and I guess I got carried away with all the filing."

"Hmm." Sharon tilted her head to the side like she was studying Barbara. "Dull weekend, or maybe you're recovering from a bad one?"

Barbara managed a tight smile. Sharon's attempts to read into her comments and actions still rankled. *Why couldn't she accept things at face value? Did she have to question and wonder about every deviation from the norm?* Barbara hoped that Sharon would leave, but the woman wasn't budging. She threw her a morsel. "Graham left for Vermont yesterday. He'll be teaching there until Christmas."

Sharon raised her eyebrows. "I thought he'd decided to spend more time creating art instead of talking about it."

The woman's razor-sharp memory never failed her. Barbara wouldn't be too surprised if she journaled nightly about all her conversations. Barbara managed a smile. "One of the instructors came down with pneumonia and decided to take an extended sick leave. No one else was available, and Graham felt guilty about disappointing the students." Last night, she had carefully rehearsed the story she would tell her friends and colleagues.

Sharon winked. "Give him some time to get settled and join him in December. That's our slow month. You could spend the entire month with him and enjoy those lovely slopes while he teaches."

"We'll see," Barbara said. No point in shooting down her suggestion and inviting more questions.

"That means no."

"Excuse me?"

"Whenever you say 'We'll see' or 'Maybe later' you're really saying no, but are too polite to argue. And that's also your way of saying this conversation is over." Sharon held up her hands. "I'm willing to sit down and listen whenever you're ready to talk about whatever is bothering you." With that, she sailed out of the room, quietly closing the door behind her.

So much for distracting and appeasing Sharon Clarke. It would be a good idea not to spend too much at the office, Barbara thought. Sharon's probing eyes didn't miss too much, and she didn't hesitate to use her questionable New Age powers to help. As it was, Barbara's schedule for the remaining two weeks in October was filled. The next time she'd have to come in was for the monthly staff meeting on the first Monday of November.

The two weeks passed by quickly. Barbara found herself putting in ten and sometimes even twelve hour days as she shuttled between seminars and workshops. Determined to distract herself, she decided to test-drive portions of the *Second Acts* series that she intended to deliver in the spring.

At the Hamilton workshop, three middle-aged women approached with expectant looks on their faces. Each woman was holding a copy of *It's Your Time*. Barbara was grateful for their nametags but couldn't really place Angela, Teresa, and Fran. She had conducted several workshops in Hamilton when she had been stationed at the west end branch and hadn't planned to return, but the organizer had been adamant and even offered to double her usual fee.

"We had to come and see you again," Fran gushed. "You inspired us at last March's workshop and that's when we finally decided to take responsibility for our lives. The next day, we made a pact to stop complaining about losing our jobs, the severance package, and everything else that was wrong with our lives."

Barbara smiled as memories of that particular workshop came to mind. She had debated about canceling when she heard the weather forecast in the morning, but in the end, she had gone. There had been over forty women at that workshop, most of them in their late-forties and early fifties. They hadn't been too happy about giving up an entire day to listen to a motivational speaker, but they had come around and Barbara believed she had made an impact.

Angela jumped in. "I still remember you staying an extra hour to answer our questions. If the hotel manager hadn't come in and warned us about the storm, you would have stayed even longer." She approached and hugged Barbara. The other women followed suit.

Tears glistened in the eyes of the three women as they continued to gaze at her.

"At first," Teresa said, "we chatted over coffee and desserts, but as soon as the weather improved, we started walking each morning and brainstorming about our futures. And when your book came out, we went through it chapter by chapter."

When Teresa paused, Angela spoke up. "We didn't realize it right away, but those walks became our first steps toward our true selves. We were no longer content to be wives, mothers, and someone else's employees. We threw out several ideas and finally decided to start our own business." She rummaged in her purse and pulled out a business card.

Barbara smiled at the name of their new business, Virtually Yours. The former administrative assistants had chosen well.

"And between the three of us, we lost a total of forty-two pounds," Teresa said. "When we hit fifty pounds, we're going on our first weekend getaway."

The three women held up their arms and clasped hands. "Montreal, here we come!"

As Barbara fingered their card, an idea popped into her head. "I would love to feature you in my *Second Acts* series. I'm hoping to release the book sometime next year. Are you interested?"

Three pairs of eyes popped. Teresa clapped her hands.

"You want to write about us?" Angela asked.

"Yes, yes I do," Barbara replied as the idea took hold. Why not include women who had benefited from reading her book and participating in the over one hundred seminars and workshops she had facilitated since joining Eagle Vision? Before leaving, Lisa738 had created a comprehensive list of all the seminar organizers and participants. And she had set up a newsletter for monthly delivery. All Barbara had to do was slip in an announcement inviting her readers to share their stories.

CHAPTER 8

Driving home, Barbara mentally thanked the three angels who had inspired her with their stories and provided another project to tide her over for six weeks. She had to somehow make it through until Christmas. Even if Graham didn't want to see her, he would want to see Gwen. Father and daughter had never spent a Christmas apart, and she couldn't imagine him breaking that tradition.

When she arrived home, she made her way up to her bedroom. As soon as she opened the door, she gasped. Annabella was floating over one of the Throne armchairs that Belinda had given her as a housewarming gift. Barbara couldn't help smiling each time she glanced at the emerald-green Caspani chairs that had cost a small fortune. Graham had been very open about his feelings. He had shaken his head and muttered, "More form than function," and shared a laugh with Paul. Both men had dared each other to sit on them while Belinda ignored their teasing. Barbara had quietly agreed but said nothing. Occasionally, she did use one of the chairs when she was putting on her shoes. As for Graham, he would only use his chair as a home for discarded clothes.

Annabella pointed at the clock. "Do you always get home this late?"

Barbara frowned. "Eight o'clock is not that late, Grandmother. What are you doing here?"

"And good evening to you, too." Annabella paused. "Belinda and I spoke earlier today."

Barbara realized that she had not spoken with Belinda

since the night of the party. Each day there was an email from Belinda filled with news of Arabella and their latest outing. Mother and daughter had covered a lot of ground since that disastrous dinner. Last weekend, they had hopped over to New York for a gala. Invitations were always extended which Barbara politely declined.

While Barbara knew she was playing right into Arabella's schemes, she felt too vulnerable to risk another meeting. To date, both encounters had gone badly and Barbara had been reduced to tears.

"You can't ignore them forever," Annabella said as she watched the changing expressions on Barbara's face. "They're not going anywhere, and if you're not careful, you will end up alone."

"There are worse things than being alone."

Annabella's lips tightened. "I can't think of a single thing."

Annabella is lonely. As this incongruous thought popped into her mind, Barbara considered Annabella's situation. Even though she was surrounded by millions of mermaids and mermen, she didn't have any close confidantes. Her position as chief elder required her to maintain certain decorum. Only with Barbara had she been able to relax. Barbara's departure had put an end to shared evenings and the Bella dynasty.

Annabella floated around the room, stopping to admire the artwork. She pointed to the watercolor that dominated the room. "He's talented and will go far." The day after he had unpacked his paint and brushes, Graham had spent the entire afternoon in the studio, capturing the beautiful autumn colors of the trees in the conservation area behind the house.

Graham's decision to sell The Art Shoppe and focus on his watercolors had released all his inhibitions. He now painted with abandon and could easily spend six to seven hours in the studio. That was, until he left for Vermont. She doubted he was doing much painting there. When he taught, he devoted himself exclusively to his students and their talents.

"When will you visit him?" Annabella asked.

"I'm booked solid until Christmas. I can't take off and go to Vermont."

"Vermont is not the moon. Book a flight and go for the weekend." Annabella smiled. "If I were you, I'd go every weekend until he agreed to see me."

"But I'm not you," Barbara said softly. She had called Graham, but she didn't feel comfortable sharing that with her grandmother. Five times she had stammered out messages that had been duly ignored.

"And you're not your mother's daughter, either." Annabella's eyes narrowed. "I sheltered you too much in the Kingdom. Your life was too simple, too easy—"

"Until you aged me thirty years and added twenty extra pounds. And let's not forget abandoning me in Carden and leaving me practically destitute."

Annabella held up her hand. "I deeply regret those moments of rage, but there's very little I can do about it now." She took a deep breath. "I'm here because Belinda and Paul are both worried."

Barbara shrugged and said nothing.

Annabella continued. "Belinda will take some kind of action and very soon. And from what I've seen of Arabella, she'll go along with it."

Barbara frowned. "What do you mean?" In her last email, Belinda wrote that she would not be returning to Canada until the spring. Memories of her one and only winter in Canada still haunted Belinda, and she had no intention of revisiting them. Thankfully, there would be a reprieve from the recent spate of mother/daughter get-togethers.

"Belinda's determined to forge some kind of relationship between you and Arabella."

"I don't want a relationship with Arabella." Barbara bit into her lower lip. "And if I recall correctly, you advised me to be careful."

"Being careful is one thing. Avoiding your mother and sister is another matter. Like it or not, you must learn how to deal with adversity."

"'Learn how to deal with adversity,'" Barbara repeated, her voice rising. "What do you think I did for most of last year?"

"No one is disputing the wonderful life you have created for yourself. But you still struggle when it comes to relationships." Annabella shook a finger at Barbara. "If you had told Graham about your mermaid past, Arabella's arrival would have had no impact on your life."

Barbara tensed. "But she and Stewart—"

Annabella floated over to Barbara and spoke sharply. "Do you still have feelings for the man?"

Barbara stammered, "No, but it's awkward. I mean, he and I, um . . ." She felt herself reddening as she recalled their lovemaking. Whenever she encountered Stewart, she tried to avoid meeting his glance. Those expressive green eyes, so similar to her own, seemed to see right through her. And Barbara still found it difficult to relax or have a normal conversation with him.

"Life is messy, both in the Kingdom and on Earth. Get used to it, Barbara," Annabella said as she faded away.

CHAPTER 9

The following morning, Barbara lingered over breakfast. Fragments of last night's conversation with Annabella raced through her mind. Intellectually, she agreed with her grandmother. Continuing to distance herself from Belinda and working long hours would not improve her situation. But emotionally, she wasn't strong enough to risk another encounter with her sister. So far, Arabella had secured five years with Lisa738, ruined Barbara's engagement party, and forged a relationship with Belinda.

As she put the breakfast dishes away, Barbara smelled those burnt coffee beans again. She frowned as her eyes traveled to the coffee maker that had been turned off. Her thoughts raced back to her engagement dinner. Minutes before Arabella's disastrous toast, she had experienced that same sensation.

What more could possibly go wrong?

As she drove into the Eagle Vision office, Barbara recalled her previous encounter with Sharon. The woman had an uncanny ability to pick up on any changes of mood or circumstances. Barbara was determined to stay clear of her. Today's staff meeting would take all morning, of that she was sure. But Barbara intended to leave immediately afterward. In the past, she often lingered over a leisurely two-hour lunch with Anne and some of the other trainers, but she wasn't up to it today.

When she arrived at the office, she was surprised to find the parking lot filled with cars. Panicking, she glanced at her watch and relaxed when she saw there was still ten minutes to go before the meeting.

Once inside, Barbara was struck by the changes in décor. Lovely flowers in varying autumn shades graced every surface and the walls had been freshly painted. An interesting shade, a neutral with subtle shades of rose or purple. Barbara couldn't imagine Sharon selecting that particular color, nor could she imagine her penny-pinching boss hiring an interior decorator. Puzzled, Barbara approached Sharon's assistant Delia, who was manning the phones. Before she could ask any questions, the telephone rang, and Delia waved her toward the conference room.

Upon entering, Barbara was surprised by the buzz in the room. Usually, everyone was quiet and subdued as they waited for Sharon to begin. But Sharon was nowhere in sight. As Barbara made her way to an empty chair, she caught snatches of conversation.

"Did you see what she's wearing today?"

"I heard her telling Delia it's a Markoo dress, whatever that means."

"And that rock on her finger must be at least five carats."

Sharon must have hired another trainer. She had been talking about hiring someone for the west end branch. She must have seen someone in action and been impressed enough to offer her the position. Much like what had happened with Barbara the previous year.

Barbara smiled as she recalled memories of her speech to a women's networking group in Carden. It was her first foray in the world of motivational speaking, and Sharon had been in the audience. Sharon had cornered her as she was leaving the hall and made all sorts of predictions regarding Barbara's relationships and career prospects. Barbara had trembled at Sharon's parting words. "The day will come, and I think it's coming soon, when you no longer feel that welcome in this small town. The universe will shake your life and force you to leave Carden."

At the time, Barbara had not been prepared to hear that her well-constructed life was about to come crashing down. It had been Barbara's first New Age experience, and she had felt so unsettled afterward. But two months later when Barbara's life spiraled out of control, Sharon was the one she called. And Sharon had come through and offered her a position as a corporate trainer at Eagle Vision.

The room quieted down. Barbara gasped as Sharon entered with her right arm wrapped around a stunning Arabella. The younger woman wore a formfitting braided leather dress. It was not a micro-mini but ended somewhere in the vicinity of the mid-thigh mark. And she was wearing stockings, sheer nightshade pantyhose with killer high-heeled black shoes that could easily belong on the red carpet. As Arabella tossed her hair, extra-large diamond studs sparkled. And of course, there was the ring on her finger that was impossible to miss, especially when it shimmered in the daylight. Other than that, no other jewelry. The makeup was very subdued. Barbara wondered if that was Belinda's influence.

Sharon beamed at Arabella, who flashed one of her killer smiles at everyone in the room. "I'm so pleased to introduce the latest addition to Eagle Vision," Sharon said. "Some of you have already had the pleasure, and I know one person who will be tickled pink to learn that Arabella Tobin has joined us." Sharon winked at Barbara. "Arabella is Belinda Armstrong's daughter and cousin to our own Barbara Davies."

Everyone clapped as the two women sat down.

Sharon continued, "A bit of background on Arabella. She comes to us from the island of Crete via California, Florida, Georgia, Texas, and too many other places to mention."

Arabella made a face. "I'm an Army brat."

"An Army brat who has distinguished herself academically. She fast-tracked through high school and has a B.A. and M.A. under her belt. In counseling psychology, no less." Sharon was practically gushing. "She was on track for a Ph.D. until . . . well, until love intervened." Sharon beamed at Arabella. "And she has decided to settle in Ontario."

Barbara simmered inside as she listened to Arabella's credentials. When she had arrived on Earth, all she had been given was a thirty-year-old philosophy degree and minimal experience in low-level jobs. How had Arabella managed to get that extraordinary skill set that dovetailed so beautifully into this job? Barbara recalled what Annabella had told her about Arabella hacking into the computer system. She must have been plotting to compete with Barbara all along. *But why? Was Arabella's life on Crete that miserable? How fortuitous for her that Stewart happened to be vacationing in Crete.*

Or maybe Arabella had planned all along to take one of Barbara's men. Graham and Andrew would have held no appeal for her. But Stewart Tobin was another story. Rich, powerful and handsome, he was the perfect match for Arabella, and he also held a grudge against Barbara.

"Earth to Barbara." Sharon's voice rang through the room. She turned to Arabella. "You cousin likes to daydream, especially during these meetings."

Arabella shook her finger at Barbara and everyone in the room laughed.

"I was telling everyone that Arabella is trying her hand at writing as well," Sharon spoke directly to Barbara. "Must run in the family."

"Are you writing a self-help book?" Anne asked.

Arabella laughed that annoying tinkle. "Oh, no. I'll leave that to Barbara." She winked at the men. "I'm trying my hand at erotica."

Sharon paused, momentarily taken aback, but quickly

recovered and got down to business. The rest of the meeting proceeded without interruption. Barbara forced herself to take notes and stay present. She hadn't realized that her daydreaming had attracted attention, and she didn't want another lightly barbed reprimand from Sharon, especially with Arabella in the room.

At the end of the meeting, Sharon winked at Arabella. "Oh, and I forgot to mention that Arabella also has decorating talents. She and Belinda decided that this office needed a makeover."

Belinda Armstrong was probably the only woman who could intimidate the usually unflappable Sharon Clarke. Barbara and Gillian had discussed this at length and concluded that thrice-divorced Sharon envied any woman who had managed to secure a wealthy and supportive husband. And while Sharon may privately gasp at Belinda's extravagance, she did respect the younger woman's taste and judgment.

"We've been telling you for years," Anne said.

"I know. I know. But Belinda Armstrong is a force, and she wouldn't let up until I gave in to her suggestions. She got me a forty percent discount on the paint and furnishings and Arabella provided the labor."

A faint blush stained Arabella's cheeks.

"Our Arabella is quite the trouper," Sharon said. "She and Belinda spent last weekend painting and rearranging all the furniture."

"Belinda painted?" Barbara sputtered. She was having a hard time believing that Arabella was capable of physical labor. But it was beyond belief to even think of Belinda holding a brush, let alone painting.

Sharon laughed. "I think she did more supervising, but Arabella was paint splattered from head to toe in her oversized overall. Her husband came and took pictures while she worked."

"What a Renaissance woman!" Ben exclaimed. The youngest of the group, Ben Elliot had spent most of the meeting admiring Arabella. He definitely had a crush on her and as Barbara glanced at the three other men in the room, she suspected they were also smitten by the effervescent Arabella. As for the women, all of whom were over forty, the feelings ranged from amused tolerance to wariness.

CHAPTER 10

Barbara was the first one out of the boardroom. The men immediately gathered around Arabella, and Barbara groaned as she heard their admiring compliments punctuated by that annoying tinkle of a laugh. Knowing her colleagues, Barbara figured that Arabella would be delayed several minutes, if not more. Enough time for Barbara to quickly check her messages and let Delia know she was leaving for the day. There was no need for her to linger and chat with the others. She already knew the main topic of conversation for the day, and it did not interest her.

As Barbara walked toward her office, she took several deep yoga breaths and tried to center herself. In this moment and for the next month, she did not have to deal with Arabella. The new trainer would be based at the west end branch, so Barbara would only have to see Arabella at district staff meetings and any social gatherings initiated by Sharon or one of the other trainers. One thing Barbara knew for sure, she would not be hosting any dinner parties that would require an invitation to Arabella.

"Barbara, could I see you for a minute?" Sharon's voice broke through Barbara's inner monologue.

Sharon and Arabella approached. The younger woman had a bored expression on her face. Sharon must have yanked her away from her coterie of admirers.

"What's your hurry?" Sharon asked, and without waiting for a reply, continued speaking. "I've decided to place Arabella at this branch. I know we need more trainers at the west end, but I think it would be better if she trained here. You can be her mentor." Sharon glanced at her watch. "I've got a million calls and emails waiting for me. I'll leave you two to sort it out."

Arabella fixed her dark pools on Barbara but said nothing. She followed Barbara into her office.

The two women were alone for the first time.

"Start mentoring me, dear sister." Arabella frowned as her eyes traveled around the room. "But I think you might need some direction first. Mama and I couldn't believe how abandoned this room looks. It's the worst one in the entire office. Even the men made some attempt at décor."

So, it's Mama now. Not Belinda or Mother or Mom. But Mama. The Mediterranean endearment that Barbara had never been able to use. She managed a tight smile. "I haven't had time to decorate. I've been busy building up my clientele."

"I can do it for you, if you want." Arabella's face took on an animated glow, and her eyes lightened as she surveyed the room. "Green, graduated shades of green. That's what I would use and maybe some rose shades. Monet or Georgia O'Keeffe prints on the wall. Light-oak furniture." She snapped her fingers. "I could have it done in a week."

"You like decorating, don't you?" In spite of everything that had happened, Barbara couldn't help putting on her career counselor hat. Even if it meant helping the sister who was trying to singlehandedly destroy the life Barbara had built for herself.

Arabella shrugged. "I like a lot of physical activity and getting my hands dirty."

"That's what you should do. Set up an interior design shop. I'm sure Belinda would help."

"Oh no you don't. You're not talking me out of working here. If it was good enough for you, it's good enough for me." Arabella smirked. "Unless you're afraid I'll outdo you.

That's a distinct possibility, you know. I'm starting out with a lot more than you had."

"Yes, yes you are." Barbara spoke slowly. She longed to ask for more details but didn't want to give Arabella that satisfaction. She already knew that Arabella had skillfully negotiated and outmaneuvered their grandmother to get what she wanted. Barbara leaned over her desk and picked up a black binder. "You can start by reading through Sharon's expectations and the history of Eagle Vision."

Arabella waved her hand impatiently. "I know all about this place and what the job entails. I have seven presentations ready to go, thanks to Lisa738."

Barbara struggled to hold back tears as thoughts of Lisa738 rushed through her mind. Lisa738 had once helped her and now she was doing the same for Arabella. Albeit, not too enthusiastically from what Gillian had said. Barbara frowned. "You don't really need me, do you?"

Arabella threw back her shoulders and gazed down at Barbara. With her heels, she was almost a head taller. "What I need is a relationship with you."

"A relationship with me?" Barbara repeated. She had been prepared for almost any response but not that one.

"That's right. BFFs, soul sisters, whatever you want to call those tight bonds these humans have."

Barbara's eyes widened. "Do you even know or understand the concept of BFF?"

"Of course, I do. A BFF is a best friend forever. You're my twin sister. You can't get any closer than that."

"It doesn't work that way," Barbara said. "You can't order up BFFs. Friends have the same value systems and look out for each other. I can't imagine you doing that for me."

"Or you doing that for me," Arabella said. "Mama's explained all the reasons you've been avoiding me, and I do understand the envy and bitterness." She shuddered. "I can't imagine losing everything like you did. I don't know what I would do. But that's neither here or there. I'm a part of your life, whether you like it or not. And I'm not going anywhere. So, you better start being nice to me."

"Are you threatening me?"

Arabella smiled and tossed her hair. "Everyone in your circle likes me. How would it look if you ignored me?"

Arabella was baring her claws. Too bad there was no audience. Barbara chose her words carefully. "It doesn't sound like you need my professional help. As for the personal involvement, I will be polite. Nothing more. Nothing less."

Arabella's eyes blazed like burning embers of coal. "You don't know or what to know what I capable of." She snapped her fingers. "I can discredit you just like that."

Barbara laughed. "Discredit me without discrediting yourself? I'd like to see you try that."

As Arabella got closer, Barbara could smell that flowery scent she had always associated with Belinda. It did not suit Arabella in the least. The younger woman needed a muskier scent, one that would blend in better with her predatory nature.

"You've already lost Graham and Gwen. Mama and Paul are on my side. Do you want to lose Sharon as well?"

"There's nothing you can do or say that will turn Sharon or anyone else in this office against me," Barbara said. "So, don't waste your breath." While she maintained a tight smile and spoke in an even tone, Barbara could hear her pulse pounding as tremors of anger shot through her limbs. She wanted desperately to sit down but would not give Arabella any more physical advantages.

Arabella smiled smugly. "Sharon doesn't like secrets or people who keep them. I wonder how she would react if I told her about your . . . *our* origins."

"You wouldn't dare!"

Arabella shrugged. "I don't care one way or another. Stewart is encouraging me to write about our lives. He thinks it has the makings of a bestseller." She laughed. "In addition to the erotica, of course."

She's bluffing. Barbara ignored the intrusive thought as memories of Stewart rushed back. He was the consummate businessman and enjoyed being on the cusp of the latest trend. His artist clients produced edgy and controversial art that had been rejected by more conservative agents. Vast stores of family money allowed Stewart to be more daring and sometimes even provocative. What could be more daring and provocative than a mermaid wife?

Barbara closed her eyes and visualized herself walking out of the office and closing the door behind her. She imagined herself waving goodbye to Delia and rushing outside to the parking lot. And then she realized that she hadn't budged an inch. She was standing there speechless and immobilized by Arabella's words. Words that could tear down her carefully constructed world and make her the laughingstock of the office. And her readers. What would her growing fan base think of a woman who was once a mermaid?

Her heart skipped several beats and she cleared her throat. She moved closer to Arabella and grabbed her arm. "You will do no such thing. Do you hear me? I won't allow it." She continued to put pressure on the arm and watched as Arabella's eyebrows rose up in alarm.

"Stop it! You're hurting me."

"Not until you promise to—"

"That will be enough," Sharon said. "Let go of Arabella at once."

Barbara released Arabella's arm and glanced at her trembling hands. She had never contemplated any violence before, and now she had been caught red-handed.

Arabella smoothed her dress and glared at Barbara as she walked by her. She slammed the door behind her, dramatically, almost theatrically.

Barbara forced herself to make eye contact with Sharon. She saw the disgust in the older woman's eyes as she pointed toward the binder on the desk. "I suggest you reread the section regarding zero tolerance for any violence in this office." She swallowed hard. "As of today, you are on a thirty-day suspension. Do not call, email, or visit during that time."

CHAPTER 11

Barbara grabbed her purse and briefcase and stormed out the door. On her way out of the building, she noticed Arabella and several trainers gathered at the reception desk. Their voices were low, but she could feel their eyes following her as she quickened her pace.

In the car, the tears flowed freely and she sat there, unable to move. Her growling stomach reminded her of the passing time. She glanced at her watch and saw that it was close to noon. It wouldn't be long before everyone set out for lunch. The thought of her colleagues seeing her weeping in the car motivated Barbara to start driving. She made it to Cobourg in record time.

Once inside the beautiful haven that she and Graham had lovingly created, the tears started again. She punched and threw the sofa pillows around the room. A pottery piece caught her eye, and she contemplated throwing it as well. Thankfully, her mood shifted.

She sat on the sofa and took out her cell phone. With shaking hands, she scrolled through the numbers. She toyed with the idea of calling Belinda and exposing Arabella, but she couldn't do that without revealing her own part in the mess. And she would bet her last dollar that Arabella had already told Belinda her version of the story. As for Paul, well, dear Paul would be sympathetic, but in the end, he would stand by Belinda.

Gillian was another possibility, but the timing was off. Gillian and Andrew were in Singapore. Barbara tried to calculate the time difference and gave up in frustration. Even if it weren't the middle of the night, it would not be a good idea to spill all of this to someone who was a continent and an ocean away.

Barbara quickly scrolled over her "human" friends, those dear people who had encouraged and supported her during her fall from grace. Mario and Nico, the gay couple who had befriended Barbara and included her in many of their outings. Elaine, the former Cardener who had given her wonderful fashion advice. With Elaine's help, Barbara had learned how to dress well on a budget. But she couldn't call any of them with this. None of them knew about her mermaid origins, and Barbara intended to keep it that way. She recalled Arabella's breezy comment about exposing them all. Stewart's fine hand was behind all of that.

Her finger hovered over Graham's number. Was he teaching? Would he return the call later? So far, he had ignored all her calls. She sighed. She couldn't handle another rejection. Especially not today.

Belinda won't allow it. Barbara smiled at the thought. Why hadn't she realized that before? There was no way that Arabella could expose just Barbara. Once she started unraveling that ball of yarn, everyone would be affected: Belinda, Paul, Gillian, Andrew, Kendra—

Kendra! The psychic ex-mermaid had been there for Barbara throughout last year's ordeal and she would be there now. Barbara was certain of it. Excited about the prospect of speaking with Kendra, Barbara dialed the familiar number and prayed she wouldn't get the machine.

"Peace and Plenty, Kendra speaking."

"It's me, Barbara. I'm . . . I'm not having a good day." She couldn't believe she had used that euphemism, but she was at a loss where to start.

"Does this have anything to do with Arabella?"

Barbara was momentarily taken aback but then realized that Kendra was well-connected with all of them.

Almost a month had passed since the aborted engagement party. Gillian or Belinda must have brought Kendra up to speed. Just as well. Barbara didn't feel like rehashing the back story. Today's events took up enough room on her overflowing plate.

"Barbara, are you still there?" There was a note of concern in Kendra's voice.

"It's gone from bad to worse." Another euphemism, but words still failed her. "Sharon suspended me for thirty days." She proceeded to give a summary of the day's events.

"Get on a plane and come down here." Kendra's voice was calm and matter-of-fact.

"I can't leave the house unattended. Graham's not here. I've got appointments. We've got workers coming next week to put in bookshelves. I have to be around in case—"

"What kind of emergency could possibly occur with bookshelves?"

Barbara burst out laughing. Kendra joined her. The mood shifted again.

"Let's start over," Kendra said. "First, are these bookshelves absolutely necessary? If you feel they are, give the contractor a key. While you're at it, give another key to a reliable neighbor or house-sitting service. You'll need someone to check the house regularly if you're going to be away that long."

Barbara closed her eyes and tried to imagine Kendra's desert community. She had heard much about Arizona but hadn't visited yet. It would be warmer, and she would be thousands of miles away from her problems. But those problems wouldn't go away.

Kendra continued, "It may sound like running away, but it isn't, you know. What you need is a change of scenery, time to sit and reflect. I don't think you've ever done that before."

"Yes, yes I have," Barbara said. "Last winter, after Graham left and I lost the career counseling job in Carden, I spent two weeks walking and skiing. When I felt more centered, I accepted Sharon's job offer."

"You have more than two weeks this time. And it's too early to ski up there. Down here, you'll have lots of opportunities to walk and hike. The weather is beautiful and I'm only a few hours away from the Grand Canyon, so we could spend time there."

"But what about your schedule?" Barbara wondered. "Don't you have clients to see?"

"I've got some flex-time. Are you coming or not?"

"I'll think about it and let you know by the end of the day." Barbara still struggled with decisions, but she had learned from Kendra that setting a personal deadline would help and wouldn't frustrate others.

Kendra laughed. "Good, you've got a little more than ten hours and I'm holding you to that timeline."

Barbara glanced around the room as she put down the receiver. With Belinda's help, she had painstakingly decorated the house to reflect her personality, as well as Graham's. The end result was a comfortable blend of muted shades and eye-popping accessories, most of them from Graham's travels. "Our forever place," Graham was fond of saying.

The phone rang. When she checked call display, she saw Belinda's number. Barbara contemplated letting the message go to voice mail, but her curiosity got the better of her. She picked up the phone and started to say hello, but was stopped dead in her tracks by the barrage of angry words that came out of the usually calm Belinda.

"I cannot believe that a daughter of mine could be so bitter, so cruel. I can only conclude that you have more of Annabella in your character. How could you even think of hurting that lovely and fragile girl who has brought only joy into our lives?" Belinda paused to catch her breath. "Have you forgotten how hard it was when you first came up to Earth? I certainly haven't and it's been over twenty years. I . . . I . . . ." She burst into loud sobs that reverberated over the telephone line.

Was Arabella some kind of demon or witch who had cast everyone under a magical spell? Barbara racked her brain for a possible explanation and could come up with nothing more than some misplaced sibling rivalry. By all rights, Barbara should be envying her sister for maintaining her spectacular Bella looks and the lottery of riches Annabella had been forced to provide.

Barbara could hear the soothing tones of Paul's voice as he calmed Belinda. Seconds later, he picked up the phone. "I don't know all the details, but I do know that Belinda is very upset. I've haven't seen her this agitated since she left the Kingdom." Barbara heard the exasperation straining his voice. "It might be best to take some distance for a while."

CHAPTER 12

It took Barbara three days to cancel the contractor, find a house-sitter, clean her house, and pack for her one month visit to Arizona. She still couldn't believe how fast she had moved after listening to Belinda's rant. Kendra was surprised but agreed that taking distance was a good idea. While she often pooh-poohed Sharon's talk of signs from the universe, Barbara was starting to believe there might be a higher power steering her away from what had become comfortable and familiar.

Comfortable and familiar. That was all she had known in the Mediterranean Kingdom. One blissful day after another, with few expectations and large blocks of unstructured time. Thinking back, Barbara marveled at the lack of meaningful activity in her mermaid life. If Andrew hadn't come along, she would have eventually become an elder but always under Annabella's supervision. Her grandmother would not have relinquished control so easily, if ever. The pleasant days would have eventually bored her to tears.

Barbara glanced out the plane window. In the past year, she had flown many times to give readings and attend conferences. Each time, she had been occupied with her notes or a speech outline. Today, she had nothing to distract her. Not even her iPad filled with the latest bestsellers could tempt her.

Barbara wasn't expecting Kendra to entertain her the whole time and hoped to complete the first draft of her manuscript. That was, if she could get past the sudden onset of writer's block. Since Monday's disturbing events, she had been unable to write a single word.

One thing did interest her, though. The desert. After spending most of her life in the underwater Kingdom, she was intrigued by the concept of dry, arid land thirsting for water. While she hadn't been able to focus on too much, she had read several travel guides about Arizona. There was so much she wanted to see and if Kendra was busy, Barbara would rent a car and visit on her own.

As her eyes flickered, visions of Montezuma Castle and enormous cactus plants drifted through her consciousness. When she woke up later, she realized they were landing in Phoenix. Barbara took out her mirror, brushed her hair, and reapplied her lipstick. She frowned at her pale reflection and the haunted expression in her eyes. Hopefully, the sun and warmer weather would give her more color and improve her mood.

As she walked through the terminal, she could feel the positive energy of the other travelers. Everyone was smiling as they pointed to the bright, almost blinding sunlit skies that awaited them outside. A welcome change from endless days of overcast skies in Ontario.

"Barbara. Barbara. Over here." Kendra's voice ran through the terminal.

Barbara followed the sound of the voice and laughed as soon as she caught sight of Kendra holding a large balloon bouquet. How thoughtful and how kind! Barbara had never received such a warm airport welcome before.

The two women hugged. Barbara's eyes welled with tears and a lump formed in her throat as she took in Kendra's twinkling blue eyes and beautiful skin. Well into her sixties, Kendra had very few wrinkles and could easily pass for a much younger woman.

Kendra patted her cheek tenderly. "It's all right, Barbara. You don't have to pretend with me or with anyone else in this state. You're a free bird here." She waved her hand. "Let those emotions out."

As they walked toward the entrance, Kendra chatted about the forecast, traffic on one of the main arteries, and plans to visit the Grand Canyon the following day. Barbara said very little until they got outdoors and breathed in the most intoxicating scent. "What is that aroma?"

"The desert air."

"It's amazing," Barbara said. The thought of breathing in that air for an entire month filled her with joy. She could actually feel her nostrils clear and lung capacity expand.

"The sun and air will cure whatever ails you," Kendra said. "I've lived here almost forty years and seen so many people at death's door miraculously come to life again. You can rise from the ashes here."

Barbara had read all about the mythical solar bird that obtained new life by arising from the ashes of its predecessors. And that's what she needed to do. Again. She had risen up from last year's debacle and she could do it again. This time, with Kendra's help.

Kendra stopped in front of a white Jeep Wrangler.

"Are you tired?" As Barbara's eyes traveled around the parking lot, she wondered where Kendra had parked. She hoped it wasn't too far away.

Kendra laughed. "This is my vehicle."

"You drive a Jeep?" After spending time with Gillian in Chicago last year, Barbara had developed an interest in cars. She read the latest *Consumer Reports* and tried to predict what people would buy. Usually, she was dead on with her predictions, but never in a million years would she have connected Kendra with a Jeep. A sports car or small sedan maybe, but never a Jeep.

"It's great on back roads and I love being higher up when I drive. It makes a difference. You'll see."

After they stored Barbara's luggage in the trunk, both women got into the Jeep. Barbara had never sat quite so high, and she found that she liked the feeling. It certainly gave her a wider range of vision, and she imagined that parking would be a lot easier. Barbara watched as Kendra expertly shifted gears and drove effortlessly along the busy freeway. Once they were out of the city, Barbara's gaze shifted to the landscape.

While she had read about the red rocks of Sedona, Barbara was unprepared for the sharp contrast between the bright blue sky and colorful terrain. And the unusual fall colors. As they drove by a canyon, she noticed the orange and golden yellow foliage. *Anything and everything is possible in this desert paradise.*

Kendra smiled as she glanced at the rapt expression on Barbara's face. The desert had already started to work its magic.

CHAPTER 13

Would the surprises never end?

After a breathtaking ride from Phoenix to Sedona, Barbara's eyes widened when Kendra pulled up to her house. "You live here?" Gillian had mentioned a million dollar house, but Barbara was totally unprepared for this magnificence. The Cape Cod style ranch house was huge, well over four thousand square feet, and surrounded by beautifully manicured gardens and a large swimming pool on what looked like an acre of land.

Kendra reached over and squeezed her arm. "Life is good, and I intend to enjoy all the abundance the universe sees fit to send my way."

No apologies. No explanations. As a well-respected psychic in demand throughout North America, Kendra could pick and choose her clients and bookings. And she wasn't afraid to charge more than the going rate. Whatever that was. Barbara tried to recall more of Gillian's comments. Knowing Gillian, she knew to the last dollar exactly what other psychics were charging and the differential that allowed Kendra to enjoy all this abundance.

To be fair, Kendra did not charge either her or Gillian for her insightful advice, advice that was always appreciated. If it hadn't been for those phone calls and Kendra's intervention, Barbara would never have extricated herself from Stewart's clutches and moved on with her life. Thoughts of Stewart segued into more disturbing ones involving Arabella. In less than a month, her twin sister had managed to destroy her well-constructed life.

Once inside, the layers of discontent and disappointment started to melt away. The house definitely had an aura about it, if it was even possible for a house to have an aura. Sharon would be able to tell her the exact color of that aura. The few times that Sharon had met Kendra, she had proclaimed to everyone within hearing that the two of them were kindred spirits. And she had deduced that both of them had yellow auras, auras of optimism and hopefulness. Thoughts of Sharon brought a frown to Barbara's face.

"What's wrong?" Kendra asked as she hugged the younger woman and brushed several strands of hair away from her face.

Barbara forced herself to smile. Sharon, Arabella, Belinda, and Stewart were thousands of miles away. There was no danger of running into any of them here. She hadn't told anyone, not even Paul, where she was going, but she had left a note for Graham on his dresser. Should he return earlier than expected from Vermont, he would know where to find her.

Kendra took Barbara's hand and led her into a chef's dream of a kitchen. The light-filled spacious area opened up into a dining room that could comfortably seat over thirty guests. Everything from the custom Shaker cabinets to the marble countertops and stainless steel appliances blended in beautifully with the calm and peaceful ambience of the place. Not even Belinda Armstrong with her designer-studded homes could boast of such a kitchen.

Kendra motioned toward one of the high chairs at the island. A wave of fatigue came over Barbara as she sat and watched Kendra assemble her blender. Kendra moved quickly and effortlessly, removing a large Tupperware container and several lemons from the fridge and two liquor bottles from a nearby cabinet. Within minutes, she created what looked like a cross between a smoothie and a martini.

Kendra smiled at Barbara's attentiveness. "All right, Miss Super Foodie. Let's see if you can figure out the ingredients in my famous martini?"

"Watermelon for sure," Barbara said as she tasted the refreshing, light drink. She closed her eyes and sighed contentedly. "Vodka, lemon, sugar and . . . and some other kind of sweet liqueur."

"Melon liqueur," Kendra said.

The two women sat quietly, sipping their martinis. As Barbara helped herself to a second martini, everyone and everything that had contributed to the past month's angst started drifting farther and farther away. She could rediscover and reinvent herself here. She was convinced of it now. Or maybe the vodka was doing the convincing.

"You're smiling again," Kendra said.

Barbara pointed to the pitcher full of martinis. "Must be some other magic ingredient in those martinis."

Kendra's eyes twinkled. "The only magic that exists is the magic you create for yourself. And I'm hoping you'll do some of that creating while you're down here."

"I don't know how I'll do it—"

Kendra put up her hand. "Set the intention and let the universe figure out the how."

"But that's the problem," Barbara said. "I don't really know what I want."

Kendra's eyes widened. "You don't want Graham back in your life?"

"This week or even earlier today, I would have automatically said yes to that. But now, I'm not so sure." Barbara's eyes traveled around the room. "To be honest, I can actually visualize myself staying here—I mean here in Arizona—for a while." During the month, she would research short-term rentals in Sedona, Phoenix, and Tucson. Much as she loved Kendra, she had no intention of overstaying her welcome.

"You can stay here as long as you want." Kendra pointed toward the staircase. "I've got five bedrooms and six bathrooms upstairs. You won't be in my way."

Barbara raised her eyebrows. "Five bedrooms?"

"I host small retreats here," Kendra said. "I have one starting on Monday."

"This Monday?" Barbara's heart sank at the thought of sharing her time with Kendra. But it was unrealistic to expect her to put everything on hold for a month. She had a business to run and her own life to lead. "I'll go sightseeing while they're here."

"No need to do that." Kendra said. "You might want to join us."

"Shouldn't you ask the others first?"

"Oh, I think the others would be more than willing. They've heard all about you from Gillian."

Barbara recalled Gillian's depressive episode last winter. She knew that Gillian had gotten help from Kendra, but she hadn't mentioned anything about a retreat. And why would Gillian share details about Barbara's life with total strangers?

Kendra reached over and patted Barbara's arm. "Relax. It's a select group of ex-mermaids who meet with me several times a year. Four of them are from the Mediterranean tribe."

Barbara perked up at the mention of other ex-mermaids. While she knew there were many of them scattered around the world, she had only met Kendra and Gillian. It wasn't surprising that Kendra would know many of them. She had been on Earth for over thirty years and had achieved acclaim as a sought-after psychic. Kendra's powers notwithstanding, it wouldn't take any new ex-mermaid too long to discover her.

Kendra smiled. "I knew you'd be happy to meet them. And I think you'll learn a lot from their human journeys." She shook her head at Barbara's raised eyebrows. "I will let them tell you all about their lives. You have a whole week to get to know them."

A week-long retreat with ex-mermaids. Barbara's mind started whirling with all sorts of possibilities—new friendships, networking, and much-needed distractions. With Belinda determined to stand by Arabella and Gillian relocating to Singapore, it wouldn't be long before Barbara would be left alone. Of course, Kendra would always be there for her, but she needed more people who knew of her origins. People with whom she would not have to pretend or watch every word and gesture. And those people could only be ex-mermaids.

As Barbara helped herself to a third martini, her eyelids fluttered and her body swayed from side to side. She imagined herself slipping away, far away from the human life she had painstakingly created for herself. She was more than ready for the next adventure that awaited her in this desert paradise.

CHAPTER 14

Simply breathtaking! There were no other words to describe the Grand Canyon. And no other basis for comparison. During her first year on Earth, Barbara had visited Niagara Falls and several other scenic sites in Canada and the United States, but nothing, absolutely nothing, could have prepared her for this natural earthly wonder.

In the Kingdom, there had been many beautiful reefs and coral formations, but all of that paled in comparison to this cityscape of landforms. And all of it painstakingly accomplished over millions of years by Father Time. Barbara smiled as she recalled the tour guide's description of a former sea bottom being forced into the sky as wind and water worked their rock-sculpting magic. What would the mermaids and mermen make of that theory?

"It had to be Eisenhower. Kennedy couldn't have done all of this during his term. He was assassinated in '63, remember?"

Barbara followed the angry male voice. It belonged to an older gentleman, well into his seventies. He was shouting at the petite woman who stood next to him.

"Of course, I remember! How could anyone forget?" While the woman was small in stature, her voice matched that of her partner. She continued, "If it had been Eisenhower, we would have heard about it long before '64. That's when the Delormes started going each year and showing all those slide shows."

"You don't want it to be a Republican, that's all. You

and your Democrats! That's who's ruining this country." The man's face was tomato red, and he was breathing heavily.

Barbara noticed several bystanders shaking their heads and smiling at the older couple. Kendra raised her eyebrows and motioned for Barbara to follow her along the trail. As they walked, Kendra spoke in a low voice. "They think the government built the Grand Canyon."

Barbara laughed. "You've got to be kidding!" She glanced at the couple who was still engaged in a heated battle.

"No, I'm not. If you think about it, it's not that naïve or preposterous." Kendra waved her hand toward the canyon. "Someone who has not traveled or read extensively could easily imagine a president or film executive actually commissioning this."

"Like James Cameron?" Barbara frowned. "I'm surprised they wouldn't think of God doing all of this." While the tour guide had shared his theories, Barbara had quietly decided this was all God's doing. A conclusion that would not even have entered her mind during her mermaid days. Barbara had been surprised by her interest in religion and spirituality. Nothing like that existed in the Kingdom. Annabella and the other elders spoke about appropriate behavior and fulfilling expectations, but there was never any reference to a higher being.

Kendra smiled. "Have you selected a faith?"

Barbara blushed. Belinda and Gillian had also been surprised by her interest in faith-based religions. It would never have occurred to any of them to attend church services. And they had conveniently attracted men who were either agnostic or estranged from their childhood faiths. "I'm still cherry picking among the different churches. To tell the truth, I haven't been too impressed by many of the priests, ministers, and rabbis in Canada."

Kendra raised her eyebrows. "You've been to a synagogue?"

"I'm open to all faiths," Barbara said. "Graham was surprised to hear that I didn't have any faith instruction. I had to scramble and say that my parents were atheists."

"Does he go with you?"

"He left the Catholic Church after his wife died and hasn't been back. He has no desire to find another faith-based religion, but he doesn't discourage me from searching."

"What are you searching for?"

Barbara stopped in her tracks. Good question. While she was drawn to both traditional religious and New Age spiritual literature, she had not yet discovered her own sweet spot on that continuum. "I'm drawn to Joel Osteen, but he's so far away." During those first few months in Carden, she had watched all of Joel's Sunday evening telecasts and had even purchased two of his books. She felt drawn to his affirmative and encouraging message.

"Houston is not that far from here," Kendra said. "We could hop on a plane and be there in less than three hours. Next weekend, I'll be busy with the retreat, but the following Sunday is wide open."

Barbara's eyes lit up. "That would be amazing." She paused. "I've been thinking about the retreat with the ex-mermaids. I want to participate."

Kendra laughed. "There you go again with all your advance planning. Why don't you wait and see how things work out? If you connect with these women, fine. If not, feel free to take off and do some sightseeing." She pressed Barbara's hand. "Don't commit to anything. Go with the flow. That's the whole point of this holiday."

Barbara frowned. "I can't waste a whole month."

"And what is it that you hope to accomplish in a month's time?"

"I need to figure out what I want and what I'm going to do about Arabella."

"I can understand figuring out what you want," Kendra spoke slowly. "As for Arabella. You really can't do anything about her."

"I have to take action. She's ruining my life." Barbara closed her eyes and vividly recalled each scene with her twin sister. Three times. They had met only three times and each time, Barbara had dissolved into tears.

"You're giving her too much power. No one, absolutely no one, can ruin your life unless you give that person the key to your inner soul." Kendra's lips tightened. "And I'm afraid that's what you have done, my dear Barbara."

Barbara was seething with anger. In the past, she had accepted all of Kendra's insights, but she was way off base today. She hadn't been there to see Arabella's smirks and contrived smiles as she manipulated everyone and everything. The others had bought into her act, even Sharon, who wasn't easily fooled by appearances.

Barbara bit her lower lip and looked toward the tall pine trees that were attempting to hide the enormous chasm. It would be wonderful to stay here amid all this beauty and not have to return to the shards of her shattered life in Ontario. There really wasn't anything there right now. Graham was gone, and God only knew if he would come back to her. Unlike Paul, she didn't possess reservoirs of patience and couldn't see herself waiting nine years for Graham to forgive her.

As for her position at Eagle Vision, did she really want to work next to Arabella, who had for some perverse reason put down roots in Ontario? And would she ever be able to have normal conversations with her colleagues? Thirty days would give Arabella plenty of opportunities to malign her to the others.

Barbara closed her eyes and tried to visualize the next five years of her life. It was an exercise she often assigned at her workshops and seminars. An activity that was well received, but it wasn't working for her now. Not a single positive image came to mind when she thought of Ontario. But when her inner gaze shifted to Arizona, she could easily visualize herself enjoying the desert sun and climbing mountains—both figuratively and literally.

Kendra watched the changing expressions on the younger woman's face but said nothing. They walked along the South Rim path, quietly taking in the magnificence that surrounded them.

Barbara's mood lifted as late-afternoon approached. Kendra broke the silence. "In another hour or so, the sun will set and we will be able to see the colors dancing along the canyon walls."

CHAPTER 15

Halfway to Sedona, Kendra muttered, "All will be well."

Barbara smiled to herself and said nothing. Knowing Kendra, she was probably blessing someone. From Gillian, Barbara gathered that Kendra's clientele was a large one, well into the tens of thousands. Her antennae were always up, and she could easily sense when one of her clients was experiencing difficulty.

"Prepare yourself," Kendra said as she pulled into the driveway. "One of the ex-mermaids has arrived a day early."

Barbara caught a glimpse of a frown on Kendra's usual tranquil features. Whoever this ex-mermaid was, she had succeeded in upsetting the calm and unflappable Kendra.

All the lights were on, and the front door was ajar. A suitcase and a large box of books blocked the entrance.

"How did she get in?" Barbara remembered Kendra locking all the doors before they left.

Before Kendra could reply, a short, curvy woman appeared at the door. She must be an Etta, Barbara thought as she took in the blond hair and soft, round facial features. While she was carefully made up, there were well-defined lines around her eyes and mouth. Barbara still had difficulty guessing human ages, but she gathered this woman was well into her fifties, maybe even into her sixties.

The woman clapped her hands and embraced Kendra. "I hope you don't mind. I've come a day early because, well . . ." She giggled. "I'm chasing a man." She pointed to the marble statue of Eros. "I found the extra key."

"Not a problem, Carole. I trust you had a safe journey." Kendra's voice was soft and accommodating. The irritability, if there had been any, had disappeared.

Carole made a face. "Lots of traffic on the I-10, but I made good time. I stopped for dinner along the way, so don't worry about feeding me. All I need is a nice bath and a good night's—" Her hands flew to her mouth. "Oh my goodness, you have a guest. Where are my manners?" She held out her hand to Barbara.

Kendra started to introduce Barbara but was cut off by Carole's scream. "Isabella! My God, it's Isabella." She hugged Barbara and stood back to admire her. "I would have recognized you anywhere. You're the spitting image of your mother and grandmother." She frowned at Kendra. "Why didn't you tell me that Isabella was joining us?"

"And what would you have done differently?" Kendra asked drily.

Barbara gave Kendra a grateful smile. She knew the older woman would not betray any of her confidences. Though, she had to admit, she was curious about Carole's romantic quest.

". . . and he's settled in the area. I'm planning to surprise him at his church." Carole waved her hand to include Kendra and Barbara. "Why don't you join me tomorrow? I checked out the location on the way here. It's halfway between Phoenix and Sedona, and it should take us less than an hour to get there."

His church. Was the man a minister? Barbara had missed the first part of the conversation and didn't want to appear too eager. Kendra had already planned their day, and she didn't want to disappoint her. In spite of that brief spat earlier in the day, she valued Kendra's opinion and goodwill.

To Barbara's surprise, Kendra nodded enthusiastically.

"I've heard of the Desertview Church community and have been meaning to drop by. Several clients have recommended it highly." She turned to Barbara. "I know you wanted to see the vortexes—"

"I can see them another time. I'll be here for a . . . a while." Barbara sensed that Carole might wonder if she heard about her month-long stay. It would be easier to let her think that she was staying for the retreat and leaving right after. Barbara was rewarded by a grateful smile from Kendra. Barbara spoke directly to Carole. "Is it a large congregation?"

"Several thousand right now, but I wouldn't be too surprised if it reaches ten thousand by Easter." Carole gushed, "David is so charismatic, so kind and considerate. He'll draw them in."

"And this wonderful man is still single?" Barbara asked.

"His wife died two years ago," Carole said. "Inflammatory breast cancer. He took it hard and retreated from everyone. This past summer, he sold the house, packed up everything, and left Texas. He decided to start over in Arizona."

Barbara wanted to hear more about this man who was reinventing himself in the desert. In some ways, his life paralleled hers, and she felt a tingle of excitement at the thought of seeing him tomorrow.

Before Barbara could ask more questions, Carole yawned loudly. "I don't know about you ladies, but I'm all tuckered out and dying to soak in a tub." She groaned as her eyes traveled to the large box. "What was I thinking when I packed all those books? I hope you don't mind if I leave them here and just take my overnight bag with me?"

"Not to worry," Kendra said. "Maria and Juanita will be here in the morning, and they'll help you get settled." She nodded toward Barbara. "I hope you don't mind if I call it a night as well."

Barbara felt her own eyelids drooping and realized she was also tired. She had slept fitfully the previous evening but knew that she would finally get a good night's sleep tonight. The first since that fateful day when Arabella had stormed into her well-ordered life.

CHAPTER 16

Barbara woke to the incessant ringing of the telephone next to her bed. Confused and disoriented, she stared at the phone for several more rings. Who would be calling her here?

She sat up and picked up the receiver.

"Good morning, Barbara. I hope you slept well. We'll be leaving for church in about an hour." Kendra hung up softly before Barbara could respond.

Barbara had planned to Google the Desertview Church, but she realized that wasn't possible. Once she got on the computer, she could easily spend an hour surfing and forget all about going to church. While she wanted to learn more about the charismatic preacher, she also wanted to see him in action. There was no time to waste if she wanted to appear presentable.

After a quick shower, her eyes traveled to the clothes in the closet. When she had packed, she hadn't considered the possibility of needing church clothes. She thought back to the small churches she had visited in Ontario and recalled a mishmash of styles. Everything from minks to jeans, stiletto heels to runners, pantsuits to cropped shorts. But this was different. From what Carole had said, the Desertview congregation was growing and Barbara was certain the auditorium would be filled with worshippers. She wished she had paid more attention to what the congregation in Joel Osteen's church wore.

In the end, she decided on her red sweater set and black print skirt with medium heels. She added her pearls and carefully applied her makeup. Satisfied with her appearance, she left her room and headed toward the kitchen.

Kendra was wearing a mauve gauzy outfit with a large colorful shawl and Birkenstocks. Carole was almost unrecognizable from last evening's tired and slightly rumpled middle-aged woman. She was pure Texas today. A large pink and black straw hat sat atop her chestnut curls and framed a heavily made-up face. She was wearing a pink boucle suit with a sheer black blouse and sheer black stockings. Her patent leather stilettos added five inches of height.

"Wow!" Barbara couldn't help exclaiming.

"Thank you," Carole said as she gave Barbara the once-over. "You look . . . nice." She quickly added, "And you too, Kendra."

Barbara wasn't too worried about her clothes. She had been fortunate enough to have a fashionista in her circle of friends. Elaine was one of the few Cardeners who had not abandoned Barbara. With a pang of conscience, Barbara realized that she had not responded to any of Elaine's calls or emails since . . . well, since Arabella arrived.

Kendra smiled and pointed toward the breakfast bar. "Help yourself to fruit and muffins, Barbara. We'll go for brunch later."

As Barbara munched on a banana muffin, she thought ahead to the service at Desertview. She had so many questions about the church and its preacher but didn't want to alert Carole, who had come early to entice the charismatic David. Carole would not appreciate any competition. Not that Barbara was interested in him. She was interested in his story, but not in him as a potential mate.

Kendra offered to drive, and Carole immediately accepted the offer. As Barbara watched Carole amble slowly toward the Jeep, she wondered how often the Texan decked herself out in heels that high. And if she had experienced any mishaps on those heels. After giving up her tail, Barbara had struggled with her human legs and had decided very early not to wear anything higher than a two-inch stacked heel.

The drive was a pleasant one with only a few scattered comments from Carole. Kendra focused on the road while Barbara feasted on the lovely scenery. She couldn't get enough of the buttes and steppes that dotted the landscape. Or the cloudless sky that added more brightness, if that was even possible, to the vivid Arizona colors.

"We're early," Carole said in a small voice as the Jeep slowed down.

"Not that early," Kendra said. "The parking lot is almost full. We're lucky if we get a spot close to the front entrance."

And what an entrance, Barbara thought. Palm trees hugged the sides of a winding road that led to the ornate doors of the otherwise plain adobe building. While it was still a work-in-progress, the potential for greatness was definitely there.

Barbara had been impressed by the interior of Joel Osteen's place of worship, but she had never seen the exterior. When she watched the telecast again, she would pay more attention to Joel's surroundings.

A deep sigh escaped from Carole. "I'm grateful, Kendra, truly I am. But I don't know . . . I mean, I can't—"

The woman had a bad case of nerves. In spite of all that show and bravado, she was petrified. Her hands shook as she adjusted her hat. Barbara leaned closer and squeezed Carole's arm. "It'll be fine," she whispered.

Kendra parked the Jeep and spoke directly to Carole. "He may not notice you or even remember you. It's been a while since he left Texas, and he departed in a cloud of grief." She waved her arm to include the property. "Making a grand entrance won't necessarily work in your favor. He might interpret that as rudeness and avoid you afterward." She paused. "But I sense there's something else here. Do you want to share now or—"

Barbara took the hint and started to open the Jeep door. "I'll go on ahead."

"Stay, Barbara," Carole said. "You may as well hear it all now. You'll get several earfuls during the retreat." She took a deep breath. "David helped me through my last divorce. And it was a messy one. He didn't see me at my best, and I guess, I'm well . . ."

"You're embarrassed," Kendra said. "As someone who has seen many clients *not* at their best, let me share something. I'm always happy when I see them thriving and flourishing. I suspect your David will feel the same."

"He's not really *my David*," Carole said. "I don't know what I was thinking. He's at least ten years younger and probably has his pick of women. Why would he even take up with me?"

Carole's sad words touched Barbara. And forced her to consider her own future prospects for relationships. If Graham didn't come back, would she start chasing younger, uninterested men or settle for older ones who may not be that exciting in bed? Or would it be easier to make her peace with remaining single?

"There's nothing wrong with wanting to connect with him," Kendra said. "It may or may not happen, but we've come this far and we're going in." She got out of the Jeep and started walking toward the entrance.

"Let's give it your best shot," Barbara said as she got out of the Jeep. In spite of her own problems, she was interested in how this would play out.

Carole reluctantly followed, stumbling several times as she tried to keep up with Barbara and Kendra. Kendra finally took hold of her arm and Barbara slowed down her pace. When they entered the building, Barbara was taken aback by the size of the auditorium. A cross between an arena and a theatre, it could seat well over ten thousand people.

An usher found them three seats in the middle section. Not the best place to attract David's attention, but it no longer seemed to matter. Carole relaxed and chatted about several of the services she had attended in Texas. As Barbara listened, her eyes traveled around the auditorium. There was definitely an air of excitement in the room. All age groups were represented. Something Barbara found surprising. When she had visited churches in Ontario, she had found herself to be one of the younger attendees. And she had listened to many sermons lamenting the lack of young people in the congregation.

SEASONS OF YOUR LIFE flashed across the four strategically-placed screens. The message alternated with beautiful landscapes and biblical quotations. While she had not read the entire Bible, Barbara recognized Ecclesiastes and felt herself relaxing.

Suddenly the lights flickered and the music started. A lovely soprano voice, accompanied by several harps, sang the hymn "All Things Bright and Beautiful" as a tall, well-built man walked purposefully toward the center of the stage. Barbara held her breath as she took in the well-styled head of hair and symmetrical facial features. The light-colored eyes glistened and a set of white, evenly spaced teeth flashed. At a distance, he could pass for JFK and perhaps that is what contributed most to his appeal. Having read several American history books, Barbara knew that Americans still revered their much-beloved president who had been killed in his prime. David held out his arms in welcome and waited for the music to stop.

"God bless you all and welcome to Desertview," his voice boomed. "Parishioners and visitors, we invite you to make yourselves at home as we join together to praise and proclaim the glory of our Lord."

As he recited the verses from the Book of Ecclesiastes, Barbara found herself mesmerized by his flawless delivery and the changing expressions on his handsome face. Charismatic didn't quite cover it. Not a single other sound could be heard as his voice carried throughout the auditorium. As Barbara glanced at the rapt faces around her, she wondered if David was casting some kind of spell on the congregation. Later, she would discuss this phenomenon at length with Kendra, who was sitting on the other side of Carole. The Texan also had an enraptured look on her face. All traces of previous worry and anxiety had dissipated.

While Barbara didn't know too much about Carole's past, she assumed the older woman had a history of relationship problems. Barbara recalled the conversation about how David had helped with her last divorce. *Just how many divorces had she gone through?* Barbara would probably hear more during the retreat.

At the end of the verses, David started on his sermon. Beautiful words spilled from his mouth and Barbara found herself nodding in agreement as she listened. Fragments reverberated through her mind. She had heard it all before, but never so eloquently. She thought of taping it, but decided she would buy the DVD later. It was far better to capture the essence of David's words rather than fiddle with electronic devices.

He ended on a dramatic note. "You are in the present season for a reason. It is your job to figure out why."

CHAPTER 17

It took almost half an hour to get out of the auditorium. Everyone was moving at a snail's pace, stopping to chat or reflect upon David's inspiring sermon. Thinking back, Barbara could remember very little of the service after David left the pulpit. Music. Dancing. Prayers. There had been a choir and several guitarists, but Barbara couldn't recall a single song they had sung. She had been transfixed by David's words and kept replaying them in her mind as she reconsidered her own circumstances.

Why was she in this challenging season? While the coming of Arabella had thrown a monkey wrench in her well-ordered life, could she continue to blame her sister for everything that had followed? When Kendra had hinted at the same thing while they were at the Canyon, Barbara had shut down and said very little to the older woman. And today, she heard the same message again. This time from a stranger, one who knew nothing of her or her past.

Barbara inwardly groaned as she realized one simple action that would have short-circuited all of Arabella's schemes. If she had revealed her mermaid origins to Graham before the day of her engagement party, Arabella's appearance would not have impacted Barbara's life. As for the incident at Eagle Vision, Barbara was to blame for losing control. She could have agreed to be Arabella's BFF but only paid lip service to that request. As all these possible scenarios whirled through her mind, Barbara wondered if some divine plan was in motion. And maybe, just maybe, hearing David's sermon was part of that divine plan.

As soon as they got outside, Barbara's eyes traveled through the mass of humanity and stopped when they reached David. Surrounded by a gaggle of women, he reminded Barbara of the many rock stars and celebrities she had watched on those red carpet events. She couldn't wait to Google David and read all about his past.

Carole groaned. "There's no point even trying to get close. We may as well leave now."

"We're not going anywhere until you make some kind of connection," Kendra said in a firm tone. "If you don't, you'll obsess about it all week and work it into every conversation. I'm not prepared to hear moans about 'What Ifs' all week. And neither are the other retreat participants."

Barbara hid a smile. Kendra certainly had Carole's number. The Texan had hoped for a spectacular entrance and some kind of instant connection with David. She had not been prepared to proactively arrange a meeting.

As Kendra started to walk toward David, Carole muttered, "That woman can be relentless."

When Barbara and Carole reached the periphery of the gaggle, they were greeted by peals of laughter. As David joined in, Barbara noted the crinkles around his reddened eyes and the forced smile that didn't quite reach his eyes. Close up, he didn't appear as attractive. Either he was under some kind of strain or the service had depleted him.

A tall, dark-haired man approached and whispered something in David's ear. David nodded slowly as his smile widened and his features relaxed. Some kind of relief had arrived.

David held up his hand. "Ladies, it's been a pleasure, but duty calls." Amid the groans, he and the dark-haired gentleman started to walk away.

"Well, there goes that," Carole said.

Barbara felt a sense of dejection as well and followed the men with her gaze. To her surprise, Kendra caught up with the men and engaged them in conversation. She pointed toward Barbara and Carole.

"Oh, my God," Carole gasped. "I . . . I don't think . . . Do I look . . .?"

"You're beautiful," Barbara said. "Let's get going before they change their minds and leave." Her heart thundered in her chest as they approached the men. The dark-haired man was pointing to his watch and whispering something to David, who was nodding slowly but saying nothing.

David started walking and met Carole halfway. "I'm flattered that you would come all the way from Dallas to hear me speak." He made direct eye contact as he grabbed both of her hands. "How are you doing?"

"Great . . . just great," Carole said. "I'm here on retreat with Kendra and Barbara. Barbara's from Canada."

David smiled at Barbara. She could feel herself tingling as his light hazel eyes locked with hers. And this time, his smile reached his eyes. "All the way from Canada." David whistled. "I'm impressed."

Barbara felt herself reddening as she held out her hand. "I was inspired by your sermon. Such a timely topic and one that gave me much food for thought." She took a deep breath and said the first thing that came to mind. "Do you have any DVDs or tapes of your sermons?"

The dark-haired man approached and gave Barbara two business cards. "You can check out David on his website. And feel free to check me out as well." He winked. "By the way, I'm Henry Whitmore, David's cousin."

More introductions were made and then Henry spoke. "I'm so sorry to break up this reunion, but we must be going. We have a lunch meeting with several ministers in Phoenix."

The three women watched as the men walked away. Carole poked Barbara. "I guess if I had to lose a man to someone it may as well be a Bella."

Barbara hugged Carole. "I'm still working on my relationship with Graham. I'm not interested in starting anything down here." There was no point denying the connection, but Barbara doubted that anything would come of it. She would order the tapes and get some kind of acknowledgement from an assistant. She doubted that David or even Henry would handle incoming orders. In spite of that, Barbara's spirits soared. It was reassuring to know that she was still able to attract another man. And in this case, a younger man. She wasn't entirely sure, but she was willing to bet that David was not yet fifty.

She was curious about Henry. "David and Henry look nothing alike. I wonder—"

"Henry is really his cousin-in-law," Carole explained. "And a distant cousin at that—third or fourth."

Even more intriguing. Not too many distant cousins maintain ties after the blood relative dies. But in this case, Barbara figured there was a financial tie that kept Henry in the picture. She had only given him a fleeting glance and could recall very little except dark hair and eyes, a well-groomed moustache, and an expensive suit.

"Time for brunch," Kendra said. "I've made reservations at the Coffee Pot Restaurant."

Carole clapped her hands. "Barbara, you're in for a special treat. Prepare to feast on the best omelettes in the state."

CHAPTER 18

Carole had not exaggerated. The extensive selection of omelettes—101 to be exact—and the ambience of the Coffee Pot Restaurant had attracted a large crowd. When the three women arrived, the interior was packed and only two outside tables were available.

The maitre'd recognized Kendra and motioned for the women to follow to one of the available tables with 'Reserved' signs. Unarguably, it was the best table on the redwood patio and allowed easy viewing of the pond, waterfall, and giant rock formation aptly called Coffee Pot Rock.

Barbara was overwhelmed by the menu, and after some deliberation selected Omelette #32 featuring avocado, mushrooms, spinach, and cheese. Kendra pointed to #75—Guacamale and Jack Cheese while Carole went for #101—Jelly, Peanut Butter, and Banana.

With so many people in close proximity, the women limited their conversation to safe topics about the weather and plans for the week. Barbara was surprised to learn the days were tightly structured with only a few outings. The sessions would start promptly at 9:00 a.m. and run until 4:00 p.m. with two breaks and a one-hour lunch. Kendra ran a very tight ship when it came to retreats.

Barbara would have preferred to linger over the rich, robust coffee and glance at the dessert menu, but Kendra made it clear they had to leave. The other retreat members would be arriving shortly, and Kendra wanted to give each woman a proper welcome.

The drive back to Kendra's house was a quiet one. Kendra focused on the road while Carole dozed off. In spite of her best efforts, Barbara found it difficult to focus on the scenery. Her thoughts kept returning to David's sermon and their short encounter afterward.

While her experiences with human males were limited, she found herself comparing David to Graham, Andrew, and Stewart. In the looks department, David was on par with the other men. A smile crept up on Barbara's face as she realized one interesting fact about herself. She was definitely attracted to handsome humans, but then, she had not met too many unattractive ones.

Personality wise, David was the most charismatic and extroverted of the group. At least that's how he appeared while on stage. Graham was content to stay in the background, and while Andrew and Stewart were dynamic in their chosen fields, they did not possess David's oratorical skills.

"We're home," Kendra said as she gently poked Carole. "Time to wake up."

The three women entered the house and found two Hispanic women scurrying about the living room. Maria and Juanita, Barbara thought to herself as she smiled at the two women.

Kendra glanced at her watch. "Everything is set to go. They should start arriving soon." She smiled at Barbara and Carole. "Feel free to rest and freshen up. We've got everything under control here."

"I could use a nice long nap," Carole said. "I barely slept last night, and I'm starting to wilt."

Barbara was glad for the temporary reprieve. When she got to her room, she retrieved her iPad and Googled David Ferguson. She had planned to quickly peruse the details of his life but ended up spending well over an hour reading several posts about the charismatic preacher.

The only child of two missionaries, he had spent most of his childhood and adolescence in third world countries throughout Africa, Asia, and Central America. David favored his mother who had retained much of her youthful beauty despite the hard and challenging life she must have led. The same couldn't be said of the dark, stern man with the dour expression who was David's father. The grim set of his features suggested a rigid, uncompromising man who had high standards and expected everyone to meet them.

Not surprising, David had rebelled and left home at age eighteen. It must have been difficult traveling solo from Honduras to the United States, but the determined young man had inherited some of his father's grit. In a few short years, he established himself in Texas.

As Barbara devoured these details, she noticed a seven-year gap between the ages of eighteen and twenty-five. There was some mention of odd jobs as a bartender, custodian, and farm hand along with part-time studies at several colleges but nothing else. Someone had glossed over these details and ensured that David emerged as an up-and-coming minister with the beautiful Miranda Young on his arm. With her heart-shaped face, shiny brown curls, and petite frame, she was the ideal companion for a young man planning to launch a ministerial career.

Barbara thought of her own human journey. Anyone who Googled her past would find very few details about the first fifty-three years of Barbara Davis's life. If someone looked too closely, she might also wonder about a woman who suddenly burst on the literary scene at age fifty-three.

He's hiding something. Something huge and potentially damaging to his ministerial career. Barbara was convinced of it, and her intuition was seldom wrong. And Miranda was the key to it. Possibly, even Henry Whitmore. All Barbara had to do was find that missing link that would connect David's difficult past to his present.

As Barbara searched for more online articles, all she could find were more glowing testimonials about David's impressive climb up the ministerial ladder. A climb that culminated with a large church and congregation in Dallas. Along the way, he and Miranda had raised three children— Peter, Sarah, and Rachel. From their birth dates, Barbara calculated that all three were young adults and nearing the end of their post-secondary studies.

After Miranda died, David retired from his church and disappeared. In all the articles, there was mention of allowing him time to grieve the death of his beautiful soul mate.

But why start again in Arizona? Wouldn't it have made more sense to simply go back to his church in Dallas? No one would have faulted him for taking so long to grieve his wife's death. So many questions whirled through Barbara's mind, and she longed to know the answers. She felt a kinship with the younger man and wanted to know more about his road to reinvention. But it would be highly unlikely that their paths would cross again. Now, if she still had Lisa738—

Her thoughts were interrupted by two soft knocks on the door. Barbara got up and opened the door to a smiling Maria. "Everyone's here, Miss Barbara. They're waiting for you."

Barbara frowned at her rumpled clothes. She needed to change and freshen up before meeting with the other ex-mermaids. She was determined to make a good first impression. While she didn't know much about them, she figured they all knew about her early struggles on Earth.

CHAPTER 19

Barbara's heartbeat picked up speed as she approached the large meeting room on the main level. She paused at the bottom of the staircase and took several deep breaths. There was nothing to fear in a room filled with ex-mermaids. Now, if they had seen her when she first arrived in England, it would have been a different story. Barbara shuddered as fragments of memories came to mind. Chopped-off dark hair. Pale skin with not a stitch of makeup. A size-sixteen body wrapped in a tight-fitting trench coat. While she had forgiven Andrew for abandoning her, she had not forgotten the horror and disgust in his eyes as he turned and walked away.

In the months that followed, she had slowly and painstakingly reinvented herself with Lisa738's help. The Numbers Mermaid had put up with Barbara's initial snubs and poor decisions. Barbara should have fought to keep her. It would have been comforting to use Lisa738 as a sounding board.

Barbara smiled as she glanced down at her outfit. The black leggings and multicolored top were appropriate for almost any occasion and gave her a lean silhouette. She mentally thanked Elaine as she confidently walked into the meeting room.

She was greeted by several gasps and appreciative murmurs. "She's gorgeous!" "A Bella, through and through!" "I can't believe she's older than I am."

Kendra approached and took Barbara's hand. "Come, you must meet everyone." She paused before a freckled brunette with dark olive skin. "This is Valerie Fraser, Arvede of the Caribbean tribe." Before Barbara could speak, Kendra moved on to a short, plump brunette. "Tamara DiFilippo, formerly Leona." Barbara smiled and then turned her attention to a tall blonde as Kendra made the introduction. "Laura Gagnon, formerly Marietta." Kendra paused. "Elsa's husband was rushed to the hospital on Friday. She sends her regrets."

Barbara committed the women's names to memory. With the exception of Carole, all were in their forties. *I can't wait to hear their stories*. It would be wonderful to compare notes and gain more insight into the struggles faced by ex-mermaids. And most important of all, it would be liberating not to worry about revealing too much of her past.

"Come, sit down," Carole said, patting the space next to her. "It's our Get Re-Acquainted Session."

"We want to hear all about the Kingdom," Tamara said. "All the juicy dirt."

"What are the Ettas up to down there?" Laura's eyes twinkled mischievously. "Any fresh scandals to report?"

Valerie winked. "Any naughty mermen?"

Barbara forced a smile as her eyes traveled around the room. While she couldn't be certain, she figured the youngest of the group was Valerie, who had probably left the Caribbean Kingdom over fifteen years ago. Barbara breathed a sigh of relief. None of them would have witnessed the preferential treatment that Barbara had taken for granted during her years in the Kingdom.

As a Bella, Isabella had not mingled with too many other mermaids. Annabella had carefully chosen her companions and closely monitored all her activities. Barbara couldn't recall a single encounter with an Etta or an Ina, let alone an Ona. Her two best friends had been Annas, only one step below her in rank. Honored to have been selected as her companions, Rosanna and Leanna were loyal to her and did not seek the company of other mermaids. The tight trio worked and played together, oblivious to the millions of other mermaids and mermen swimming around them.

Each year since turning eighteen, Barbara had been crowned Most Beautiful Mermaid at the Summer Solstice Celebration. While no one competed against her, there was healthy competition for the two runner-up positions. Barbara winced as she recalled the months of preparation that went into the annual celebration. All the other mermaids had been expected to volunteer at least two days of work. Only Annabella and Barbara had been exempt from this ruling.

As for the mermen, they kept their distance and nodded respectively. There was cavorting among the mermaids and mermen, but it was far removed from Barbara. She tried but couldn't recall the name of a single merman. What on earth could she say that would satisfy the curiosity of these women?

Kendra came to her rescue. "Let's give Barbara time to catch her breath."

Barbara flashed a grateful smile as she leaned back and listened as the others provided updates on the previous year. Barbara's eventful year paled in comparison to the drama that quickly unfolded.

Carole's fourth husband had declared bankruptcy and left the country with his nubile young assistant. The older woman's lips quivered as she described that stressful first month when she had found herself alone with closed bank accounts, canceled credit cards, and a mountain of unpaid bills. Carole had been forced to sell the heavily mortgaged monster home and rent a modest apartment on the outskirts of Dallas.

Tamara was still married to her third husband but dealing with a stepson who spent his days sprawled on the couch in the family room and a stepdaughter who had moved back home with two children, one of them a toddler. Tamara sighed longingly as she described the short-lived empty nest that was now crammed with too many people and too many issues.

Laura smiled guiltily as she described her recent wedding to Husband #2. While she didn't give too many details about the gentleman, it sounded like he was at least a decade older. There were grandchildren and great-grandchildren that Laura occasionally babysat, but she didn't seem to mind.

Barbara was surprised to hear that Valerie had never married and was content with short-term relationships that didn't last longer than a year.

After dinner, Barbara excused herself and went upstairs. She took out Graham's picture and placed it on her dresser. It was time to take more action. She did not want to end up alone like Carole or content with flings like Valerie. The phone calls were not enough. Knowing Graham, he was deleting them without even listening to the message. Barbara took out her iPad and started writing.

To: Graham
From: Barbara
Re: Us
I miss you. Not a day goes by that I don't imagine your beautiful face or recall one of your witty comments. While we haven't been together for too long, I know that I want to spend the rest of my life with you, and only, you.

I've made mistakes, big mistakes. I should not have slept with Stewart, accepted the car and, worst of all, conceal my mermaid past from you. When I finally told you the truth, I could see the anger and hurt lurking in your eyes. And the question that I could not answer myself: Why did I wait so long?

Even now, I struggle with that answer. I was afraid you would look at me differently and reject my past. Having been abandoned by Belinda and Andrew, I didn't think I could handle another rejection.

I don't expect you to forgive me right away, but I would like to open the lines of communication. I'm visiting Kendra in Sedona and will be here for a month. I would love to hear from you.

Love,
Barbara

CHAPTER 20

The next morning, the retreat started promptly at 9:00 a.m. Kendra made her way to the front of the meeting room where an old-fashioned blackboard had been set up. After a brief welcome, Kendra wrote the following question on the blackboard: *What have you outgrown in the past year?*

Not certain how to respond, Barbara watched as the other ex-mermaids picked up their journals and started writing. After a few quiet minutes, Barbara followed suit and recopied the question. Without too much thought, she wrote: *Eagle Vision.* Surprised by that unexpected response, Barbara dropped her pen. That wasn't what she had planned to write. But it was her first response and it was definitely unfiltered. She continued to gaze at those two words and was startled by the sound of Kendra's voice. It was time to move onto the next question. As Barbara picked up her pen, she noticed that Valerie had filled up two pages of her journal.

The second question was equally provocative: *Are your priorities too comfortable?* Audible sighs filled the room. From what Barbara had heard the previous day, she suspected actual comfort was desired but in short supply. Barbara toyed with her pen as she considered her relationship with Graham. *Was that too comfortable?*

Safe. Dependable. Secure. Those were the adjectives she had first associated with Graham. And she had taken him for granted, assuming he would always be there to pick up the pieces. Those three months they had spent apart had been difficult ones, but with help from Sharon and Lisa738, she had launched a successful career as a corporate trainer. *Back to Eagle Vision.* She had definitely been comfortable there as she watched her salary climb into the six digits.

More questions followed and Barbara found herself filling up her journal pages with mostly unfiltered thoughts. By noon, she knew that she would be fully participating in all the week's activities. In the afternoon sessions, they broke off into pairs and triples and discussed the morning's journal entries. The other ex-mermaids were all fascinated by Barbara's story, and several pairs of eyebrows were raised when Carole exclaimed, "Three men in one year!" They all gasped at the thought of receiving only a check for ten thousand dollars as compensation for Andrew's abandonment.

"You should have demanded more," Laura said. "He had a responsibility to support you for at least a year."

Barbara had been surprised to learn that newly-arrived mermaids were given generous allowances well in excess of five thousand dollars a month and several gold-plated credit cards. The other ex-mermaids seemed aghast at the thought of surviving on less than one thousand dollars a month.

The following day, more questions appeared on the blackboard. The focus was still on comfort, or more precisely, getting out of comfort zones. As Barbara watched the changing expressions on the faces of the other ex-mermaids, she suspected the topic was hitting several nerves. Barbara was also starting to feel uncomfortable with the topic.

Barbara marveled at Kendra's facilitation skills. No notes. No pauses. Simply a constant and gentle flow of questions and insights. In addition to writing her own responses, Barbara paid special attention to how Kendra structured each session. She would definitely incorporate Kendra's techniques into future seminars and workshops.

Barbara found herself most drawn to Valerie. She enjoyed the younger woman's witty and sometimes outrageous comments. At first, Barbara was shocked by the multiple F-bombs that were dropped in all conversations but soon became immune to them. While her own issues still remained, Barbara started imagining a different kind of life, one without a permanent man but filled with supportive girlfriends. BFFs. Her expression hardened as she recalled Arabella's arrogant request.

"Stop scowling," Valerie said. "You'll end up with wrinkles and drive all the men away."

Barbara laughed. "No one left to drive away. They've all moved on."

"And so can you," Valerie said.

They were sitting on the back verandah, apart from the others. They were supposed to be role-playing, but Barbara wasn't worried. While she had completed most of Kendra's exercises, she found that whenever Valerie was her partner, the conversation headed in a different direction. Afterward, Valerie would come up with an amazing summary for the group.

Barbara's eyes traveled around the beautifully manicured garden. While she recognized several cacti and succulents, she could only gaze in admiration at the other colorful flowers with such unique names as scarlet creepers and globe mallows. She closed her eyes and imagined living in a small bungalow or townhouse with its own flower garden. Relocating to Arizona wouldn't surprise anyone who had read her bio. Barbara Davies had lived in Tempe until her philandering husband left her for a nubile personal assistant.

Before leaving for Arizona, Barbara had Googled Carl Davies and scrolled through several pages of entries before discovering he had died two months prior to her arrival on Earth. All the details had matched: he was recently divorced and had retired his professorship at Arizona State. There was no mention of another relationship or any other family, for that matter. It was the perfect identity for a newly minted ex-mermaid planning to reinvent herself in Canada. Barbara doubted that any of the Cardeners had probed too deeply into her past. Sharon was the only one who might have dug a little deeper.

Each day, it was becoming easier and easier to leave Canada behind. As for her job at Eagle Vision . . . That was becoming less and less desirable. Could she return to an office where everyone knew about her altercation with Arabella? And more importantly, could she work alongside a narcissistic sister who was hell bent on destroying her life?

"Earth to Barbara," Valerie said as she waved her hands frantically. "Where did you go?"

"Canada," Barbara whispered. "I don't want to go back."

"Don't." Valerie gestured around the property. "Stay here until you know where you want to go. Kendra won't mind. She's put up each of us for different periods."

While that was definitely a possibility, Barbara knew that she could not stay here indefinitely. When Kendra had issued the invitation, she had specified a month. In addition to her generous nature, Kendra also possessed the ability to set effective boundaries.

The tinkle of a bell signaled the end of the session. Valerie winked. "I'll do the honors."

Barbara shook her head as the two women walked toward the meeting room. "I don't know how you come up with all those summaries. It's like you've prepared beforehand."

"In a way, I have. Ten years of therapy have given me enough insights for two lifetimes."

Barbara's eyes widened at the thought of all that therapy. And the expense. But it didn't sound like Valerie was hurting for money. Her men had provided for her. None of her investments had been touched by the recession, and she lived securely in her mortgage-free house in Albuquerque.

The others were not as fortunate. Having been promised a life of riches and leisure, they were not too happy with the prospect of living more frugally. Barbara wasn't that overly concerned about money. She appreciated the abundance that surrounded her, but she could manage very well on less. And if Graham decided not to marry her, she would have to scale down her lifestyle considerably. Unless she wrote more prolifically and produced books that reached bestseller status.

On their way to the meeting room, Barbara and Valerie noticed the other women gathered around Kendra, who was holding a large bouquet of red roses. Barbara groaned inwardly as she recalled the large bouquets she had once received from Stewart. It was hard to believe that less than a year ago, she had actually considered a life in Chicago.

"Barbara, you have an admirer," Kendra said as she handed the flowers to Barbara.

Were they from Graham? Had he read her email? Was he hoping to reconcile? Her heart quickened as she threw the roses into Valerie's arms and opened the envelope. She gasped at the name. *David Ferguson.*

"Who is it?" Kendra asked. The others huddled around and gave Barbara no choice but to share the news.

While Valerie, Laura, and Tamara awaited an explanation, Carole's cheeks flushed pink. "I'm not surprised. You two made an instant connection on Sunday."

"David? David the preacher?" Valerie raised her eyebrows as she turned toward Carole. "*Your* preacher?"

"He's not my preacher or my anything else," Carole said.

Barbara caught the glances exchanged by the other women. While Carole had simply glossed over the details of Sunday's meeting with David, there was definitely more of a history. Or an imagined history on Carole's part. David had been happy to see her, but he had not displayed any romantic interest. And Carole had appeared quite content to not pursue the matter any further. At least she did on Sunday.

Maria appeared with two vases. "Which one would you like?"

CHAPTER 21

The rest of the afternoon dragged, and Barbara wished she could sneak away and collect her thoughts. David's extravagant gesture had left her unsettled and uncertain about how to proceed. With Stewart, there had been no hesitation. She made it clear that she wanted more time to think about their relationship. Not that it had made any difference. Stewart had ignored her pleas and continued to shower her with unwanted shows of affection.

She longed to take Kendra aside and get her advice, but Barbara would have to wait until the end of the session. There was no way that Kendra would skip any portion of the retreat activities. And Barbara did not expect any special treatment that could antagonize the others. Since Sunday, Kendra had spent no one-on-one time with Barbara. While she had greeted her every morning, Kendra had not gone out of her way to engage in conversation. And Barbara had respected that boundary. After all, the other women had paid to be at the retreat.

Barbara barely listened to the other presentations but forced herself to pay attention when Valerie stood. The younger women tossed her black curls and winked mischievously at Barbara. She proceeded to describe three conclusions they had reached during their role-playing exercise.

Unbelievable. It was uncanny how Valerie was able to deliver such an eloquent summary of a conversation that had never occurred. Barbara wondered if this was one of

Valerie's Specialist Skills. Barbara would have to find out later which Skills Valerie had requested and received.

Afterward, the women gravitated toward the back verandah where pitchers of watermelon martinis and platters of fresh fruit awaited them. Barbara caught Kendra's eye and motioned toward the front sitting room.

When the two women were alone, Barbara spoke. "I don't know what to do, Kendra. Do I call him? Send a thank you note?"

Kendra held up her hand. "Before you do anything, I think you should know that Henry delivered the roses."

Taken aback by the revelation, Barbara simply stared at Kendra. The older woman frowned as she said, "I had some time to check out Henry while you were in the small groups." She paused. "Henry handles all the details of David's life and makes sure that everything runs smoothly. He's the one who introduced David to Miranda, and I wouldn't be too surprised if he has anointed you as the next Mrs. Ferguson."

"But why couldn't David send the flowers? If he's interested, and I think he is. At least, it seemed that way on Sunday."

"I imagine that David expressed his interest and Henry agreed to help with . . . with the courtship."

"The courtship?" Barbara's eyes widened. "You've got to be kidding." After a very short encounter that lasted less than five minutes, Henry had concluded that David and Barbara were destined to be soul mates. Could they really be having this conversation in 2014?

"I wish I were." Kendra raised an eyebrow. "How do you feel about David?"

"I guess I'm flattered by his attention. And I have to admit there was definitely a connection on Sunday and—"

"And you wouldn't mind dating him for a while and building up your confidence," Kendra said.

Barbara took several deep breaths and analyzed the situation. It wouldn't hurt to go out with David. She could send a thank you email and give David a chance to check with Henry. And then, well, she would wait and see.

"You've decided to pursue this," Kendra said.

"Yes, yes I have. I have no intention of committing to any long-term relationship, but I wouldn't mind a short . . . um—" She had sent the email to Graham two nights ago and received no response. Had he even read it? Barbara didn't know what to think anymore. While she had not expected any kind of response from David Ferguson, she was intrigued and flattered by his interest.

"A fling," Kendra said. "A fling with the preacher."

Barbara winced. "I don't like the sound of that."

"Then don't have a fling." Kendra walked toward the back verandah, leaving Barbara alone with her jumbled thoughts.

"I wouldn't worry too much about getting Kendra's approval or anyone else's for that matter." Valerie approached and winked at Barbara. "If you want to have a fling, go ahead and have it. Best way to recover from a break-up."

Barbara frowned. "I'm not really sure that Graham broke off—"

"Honey, he left the engagement party without saying a word, and he left a note for his daughter to deliver. No emails. No phone calls. No letters. And even worse, he didn't respond to any of your calls. I've only dated a couple of Canadians, but I'm pretty sure that behavior classifies as ending a relationship in any country."

Barbara stared at Valerie open-mouthed, momentarily stung by her remarks. The younger woman's assessment seemed so cold and clinical, but she was right on the money. Over a month had passed and still no word from Graham. If there was any hope for future happiness, she had to sever herself from Graham and move forward. And she had to start now.

Valerie whispered. "Call the preacher and thank him for the flowers."

"I was going to email—"

Valerie shook her head emphatically. "He gets hundreds of emails and probably has a gatekeeper dealing with them. It could be days before he responds. You don't have that kind of time."

Valerie and the others had assumed she would be leaving on Sunday, and Barbara had chosen not to enlighten them. She didn't want them to think she was getting preferential treatment. As it was, they already knew she hadn't paid for this very expensive retreat.

Barbara had still not recovered from learning that Kendra had charged each woman two thousand dollars. It sounded like an exorbitant fee to charge, but the other ex-mermaids had assured her they were getting a reduced rate. One of them, Barbara couldn't remember which one, had suggested that Barbara present Kendra with an appropriate gift before leaving. Now that she knew the going rate, she felt even more uncomfortable.

Barbara made her way to her room. Once there, she searched for David's card and located the number for Desertview. With her heart pounding and hands trembling, she dialed the number. While waiting for the machine or one of the gatekeepers to pick up, she mentally composed the message she would leave.

"Good afternoon, David Ferguson here."

Barbara had not expected a busy preacher to pick up his phone.

"Hello, is anyone there?" David asked.

"Um . . . It's Barbara. Barbara Davies calling."

"Barbara! How wonderful! I was hoping to hear from you."

Barbara regained her composure. "Thank you for the lovely roses. It was so kind of you to send them."

There was a small pause. "Uh . . . yes, I'm so glad you like them."

Barbara smiled to herself. Henry had not updated him, but it didn't really matter. He sounded happy to hear from her.

David cleared his throat. "I have a breakfast meeting in Flagstaff tomorrow morning. If you're free, I could pick you up on my way back home. Let's say around eleven. I don't know how much sightseeing you've done. We could have lunch and visit one of the vortexes."

With a pang, Barbara realized that she would be missing the third day of the retreat. Kendra would not be too pleased and the others, especially Carole, might be envious. She had picked up a vibe downstairs, and she wasn't sure how to proceed.

"Barbara. Barbara. Are you still there?" David sounded anxious. "I hope I haven't come on too strong."

"No, not at all. I haven't seen any of the vortexes and would love to see them with you."

As Barbara hung up the phone, a sweet lavender scent flooded her nostrils. A bit strong but still pleasant enough. She hummed to herself as she examined the clothes in her closet. What would she wear for her first date in Arizona?

CHAPTER 22

Barbara woke up to the sounds of waves crashing on the shore. She was surrounded by large, dark rocks and a murky, ominous sky. The locale was strangely familiar as she tried to find her bearings. She shivered and hugged the thin blanket wrapped round her. When she turned to her right, she saw Annabella perched on a nearby rock. Barbara had been transported to Malta.

Annabella sighed deeply. "We need to talk."

"And we couldn't have done this in Sedona?" Barbara asked.

Annabella's eyes widened. "With five ex-mermaids in the house and one of them a witch?"

"She's not a witch. She's a psychic and . . . and she's been helping me." At least Kendra had helped her in the past. But lately, the older woman had started to take distance. Or maybe it seemed like that to Barbara. This week, four other ex-mermaids competed with her for that attention. But Kendra's disapproval of a possible relationship with David was clear. Since yesterday's conversation, Kendra had barely smiled in her direction.

"I would have helped," Annabella said. "All you had to do was ask."

"I'll keep that in mind for the future." Barbara huddled within the blanket. She had forgotten how cold those late-November evenings could be.

Annabella smiled. "I had considered bringing a warm coat, but I remembered how quickly you disposed of my last gift."

When they had met on this shore in January, Annabella had provided a coat of animal skins that Barbara later learned was mink. Expensive mink. Chocolate-brown luxurious mink. Within days, Lisa738 had sold the coat and deposited a hefty sum in Barbara's account. Barbara shivered. "A warmer blanket would have been nice."

Annabella laughed. "I'll keep that in mind for the future." She reached down and picked up a shiny rectangular object.

Barbara gasped. It was a tablet. While other ex-mermaids would be jumping for joy, Barbara felt only a profound sadness. She would have to start over with another Numbers Mermaid who wasn't Lisa738. There would be benefits and access to more Specialist Skills, but it wouldn't be the same. "Thank you, Grandmother. But I don't really need—"

Annabella held up her hand. "I'm including Lisa738."

Barbara let go of her blanket. Her hand trembled as she accepted the tablet. "How is that possible?" Barely two months had passed since Arabella had announced that she had five years of online mermaid support with Lisa738.

Annabella's lips tightened. "Both parties agreed to end the relationship, and I was more than happy to oblige them." Her shoulders sagged. "From the start, Lisa738 complained about Arabella. Her demands. Her condescending manner. And the daily reprimands and put-downs."

"Daily reprimands and put-downs," Barbara repeated. She couldn't believe what she was hearing. She thought back to how tirelessly Lisa738 had worked on her behalf. And she had even volunteered to perform extra tasks. She was no slouch and whatever Lisa738 thought of Arabella, she would not skimp on her duty. It was that ingrained within her.

"Arabella was raised very differently from you, from all the other mermaids in the Bella tribe. She never felt valued or loved." A tear slid down Annabella's cheek. "I didn't realize . . . No, I chose not to see Sarabella's neglect and mistreatment."

It was the first time her grandmother had taken responsibility for her actions. And it was a shocker. But Barbara could not disagree. If Annabella had not banished Sarabella and Arabella to Crete, so much unhappiness and strife could have been prevented. She could have intervened at any time during the past twenty-four years and whisked Arabella back to Malta where she would have shared in the Bella bounty. But there was no point crying over that now. Barbara walked over and hugged Annabella.

The mermaid clung to her tightly and sobbed quietly. Annabella pulled away first and managed a smile. "You . . . you're the one I miss the most. You're the child of my heart, the love of my life. I know I treated you badly, but I want to make amends." She wiped away her tears. "As long as I am able, I will do whatever I can to make your life on Earth more pleasant." She pointed to the tablet. "I have given you five years of online mermaid support."

Five more years with Lisa738. It was beyond wonderful. But she was still confused. "I'm grateful, Grandmother. But how did you persuade Arabella to give up Lisa738?"

Annabella shrugged. "That was simple. Yesterday, Arabella demanded to see me and when I arrived, she had a laundry list of complaints. All pettiness and nothing worth repeating, so I will spare you those details. When I offered her another Numbers mermaid, she immediately accepted."

While Barbara was shocked by Arabella's treatment of Lisa738, she wasn't surprised. It wouldn't be too long before Arabella revealed her true colors to Sharon, Stewart, Belinda and anyone else she had charmed. Barbara had never been on the receiving end of that charm and neither had Annabella.

"Be careful," Annabella said. "She envies you. You were the perfect Bella, the chosen one."

"But so was Belinda."

"She knows that Belinda fought to keep her. And that is enough for now."

Those last two words stopped Barbara cold. The day would come when Arabella no longer needed to be in the good graces of Belinda Armstrong, and when that day came, the relationship would end badly. Barbara shivered.

Annabella reached over and stroked her arm. "I won't keep you much longer. There's one other thing you should know." She swallowed hard. "This may be the last time I see you."

"What are you saying?" Barbara took a closer look at her grandmother. Well into her seventies in human years, she could easily pass for a twenty-five-year-old. While mermaids collected the years like humans, they did not show their ages and they maintained excellent health throughout eternity. But once a mermaid gave up her tail and assumed human form, the aging process began.

"There will be an election this coming Saturday," Annabella explained. "I may lose my position as chief elder."

"But how is that possible?"

"I've been chief elder for almost fifty years, longer than any other elder in the entire Kingdom. For the past few months, there have been rumblings among—"

"Sarabella?"

"No, I've got her under control. And even if she did try to usurp my position, the others wouldn't allow it. Many of the mermaids are tired of the Bella reign and they want change."

Barbara couldn't even fathom another tribe gaining power. During her twenty-three years in the Kingdom, all she had known was her grandmother's rule. And she had assumed that everyone liked it that way. Annabella calmly settled all disputes and had weekly open sessions where she welcomed input from everyone, even the lowliest of mermaids and mermen. When someone had to be disciplined or banished from the tribe, she deliberated for days.

Barbara frowned. "Who could possibly take over? No one is trained for leadership." After her mother had left the Kingdom, Annabella had pinned all her hopes on her granddaughter. At her quarter-century celebration, Barbara would have assumed Annabella's position. But with her gone, there was no direct line of succession.

"That's not stopping any of them from trying." Annabella's jaw clenched. "A couple of Inas are itching for my job, and they put their names forward."

Barbara shook her head. "Not a single Ina comes to mind."

Annabella managed a smile. "Kendra was an Ina."

"But she's different."

"Not really," Annabella replied. "She achieved that success on Earth mainly because she applied that enterprising Ina spirit and chose her Skills wisely."

Images of Ina markets came to mind. Whenever Barbara had wanted to trade or barter goods, she would visit their stalls and bargain with them. While she got what she wanted, it was always at a higher price. With her focus entirely on the item, she rarely made eye contact with them but occasionally she noticed strained smiles, raised eyebrows, and bored expressions. She thought of Inas mainly as a means to an end. An attitude that she had picked up from Annabella who was probably the only mermaid who got what she wanted at *her* price.

"Two of Kendra's cousins want the position. And they may get it."

"Unless you take proactive measures." Barbara realized she didn't want to lose touch with her grandmother. Only elders were allowed to travel between Earth and the Kingdom.

"What could I possibly do in less than a week?" Annabella's voice quavered.

"Present them with an alternative for the future. Offer to train a prospective candidate."

"There's no one to train," Annabella sputtered.

"How about Leanna and Rosanna?" Barbara smiled as she recalled her BFFs in the Kingdom. Born within days of each other, the two sisters and Barbara had formed a tight bond, one encouraged by Annabella.

Annabella frowned. "They have no bite."

"Neither did I," Barbara said.

"I would have helped you develop that bite," Annabella countered. "I had planned to start including you in council meetings but—"

Barbara bowed her head. When she had met Andrew, she had thought only of spending the rest of her life with him. While she remembered little of the transformation process, she did recall Annabella's harsh words beforehand: "Do you know what giving up your tail means? It means that someday, someone less worthy will assume leadership of this tribe."

That day was rapidly approaching and unless Annabella accepted the possibility of change, she would not fare too well in the new regime. Barbara cleared her throat. "Leanna and Rosanna were always very supportive of you. I don't imagine that's changed." Barbara watched as Annabella slowly nodded in agreement. She continued, "If one of them assumes leadership of the tribe, she will take care of you." As a past elder, Annabella would eventually retire to the island of Corsica. There she would join the retired elders of all the tribes. With Leanna or Rosanna at the helm, she could look forward to regular visits and gifts. If someone else assumed leadership, she would have no contact with the tribe and lose face among the other elders.

Annabella frowned. "But which one do I select?"

"Train both and let the tribe choose."

Annabella's face softened and her eyes glistened with tears. "I am so proud of you, granddaughter." She spread out her arms and welcomed Barbara into an embrace. They sat there for several minutes, not speaking but simply basking in each other's love.

CHAPTER 23

When Barbara woke up the next morning, the flickering of a green light caught her attention. She jumped out of bed and touched the green light. The blinking stopped and a smiling face materialized on the tablet.

Lisa738.

For several minutes, no one spoke. Barbara's eyes welled with tears as she gently stroked the tablet. Their fingers met.

Barbara broke the silence. "I am so glad to see you. You have been in my thoughts since we parted."

Lisa738 nodded. "I'm here for you. Let me know what you need and I will get it for you."

There really wasn't anything she desired, but she was curious. "I'm wondering about Arabella—"

Lisa738 burst into tears and sobbed quietly before swallowing and regaining her composure. "I'm sorry, Barbara. But you'll have to get the details from someone else." She pointed to Barbara's laptop. "If you check your inbox, you'll find an email from Gillian." She waved goodbye and faded away into the screen.

Barbara had hoped for a longer conversation, but it was obvious that Lisa738 still hadn't recovered from Arabella's mistreatment. Barbara placed the tablet on the night table and picked up the laptop. Sure enough, there was a message from Gillian.

To: Barbara
Re: Sister Dearest
Where are you??? I've been calling your cell and leaving

messages. And so has Belinda. She called me yesterday, frantic with worry. And then she broke down and gave me the latest update in the Arabella saga.

Arabella managed to get herself fired. Your boss found her in a compromising position with one of your colleagues. And get this . . . they were in your office!

I'm not really sure what they were doing, but it must have been pretty serious for Sharon to take such drastic action. Before Arabella could spin her own tale, Sharon phoned Belinda. Mother and daughter hashed it out and concocted a story for Stewart. I don't know for sure but I imagine Paul was also involved in the subterfuge.

Arabella must have put on quite a show, maligning Sharon and hinting that she was pressured to quit. Stewart was incensed and ready to call an employment lawyer. Arabella managed to calm him down but, unknown to her, he decided to visit Sharon and demand she reinstate Arabella.

I would love to have been a fly on the wall when Sharon enlightened him. And it doesn't stop there. When Stewart returned home, he found Arabella flirting with Sammy, Gwen's husband. Belinda bought Arabella's story that Sammy was just comforting her, but that's not how it appeared to Stewart. Sammy ended up with a black eye and confessed everything to Gwen.

Belinda broke down again and Paul got on the phone. I don't think he was too pleased with all the confidences she had shared, but he did ask me if I knew your whereabouts.

You might want to connect with Belinda and Sharon. AND TURN ON YOUR PHONE!!!

XOXO Gillian

Barbara reread the email several times, each time focusing on a different section. She could easily imagine how distraught Belinda would be to learn that Arabella had cheated twice on Stewart. While no name had been mentioned, Barbara had a strong feeling that Ben Elliot was the other man at the office. She wondered if Sharon had also fired him. If she had, that would have been devastating for Ben and his wife. Heavily mortgaged and expecting their third child, they could not afford to lose his six-figure paycheck.

Barbara's insides were churning as visions of Arabella and Ben having raunchy sex in her office came to mind. And all initiated by Arabella. On his own, Ben would never have suggested using Barbara's office as their love nest. Barbara knew then that she would not be returning to Eagle Vision at the end of her thirty-day suspension.

The flickering of the green light caught her attention. Lisa738 had regained her composure and was ready to speak. How admirable of her to demonstrate loyalty toward Arabella. Barbara doubted very much that Arabella was maintaining any form of decorum. In less than two months, she had maligned and upset Lisa738, tempted two married men, and driven her sister away.

Barbara tapped the green light and waited for Lisa738 to appear. Her eyes were shining and all traces of tears had disappeared. Barbara decided to close the chapter on Arabella and focus on her own life. She gave Lisa738 a quick rundown of yesterday's events involving David Ferguson and Henry Whitmore.

Lisa738's eyes welled with tears. "So, it is over with Graham."

Barbara spoke more briskly. "I'm not looking for a long-term relationship." She winced as thoughts of Henry's anointment came to mind. "But I think David and Henry may have other expectations."

"I'll investigate both men thoroughly and have a report ready for late this afternoon." Lisa738 paused.

Barbara wondered about her thought processes. The Numbers Mermaids were trained to think and act logically.

All left brain with very little sentiment. But Lisa738 had a well-developed right brain that sometimes interfered with her rigorous training. Barbara suspected that Lisa738's affections still lay with Graham. How Barbara wished that she had arranged a meeting between the two. Lisa738 had hinted right until the end, but Barbara had not been ready to reveal her past to Graham. And that reluctance had cost her dearly.

Lisa738's face lit up. "One more thing. Annabella has given me permission to grant you a fourth Specialist Skill. You have until—" Her expression changed.

"Until Saturday," Barbara finished. It didn't bode well for Annabella if Lisa738 thought her leadership would end this coming weekend. As a Numbers Mermaid, Lisa738 would have access to all poll and survey results. In the past, polls had been commissioned for any new initiative. The first election in almost five decades qualified as a new initiative and would certainly merit several polls. Barbara hoped that Annabella would take her advice and approach Leanna and Rosanna. That last-minute gesture could dramatically swing the vote in her favor.

"Saturday at midnight," Lisa738 stressed.

Right now, a fourth Specialist Skill was the last thing on her mind. But she would give it considerable thought after her date with David. If nothing came to mind, she would ask for financial acumen, a Skill that would come in handy during her unemployment.

CHAPTER 24

David was ten minutes early. Thankfully, there was no one around when he rang the bell. Barbara had already had a one-sided conversation with Kendra who simply nodded when Barbara informed her she would not be participating in today's retreat. During breakfast, Barbara had said nothing to the others and returned to her room as soon as she finished eating. It was the cowardly way out, but she didn't feel like talking about her date with David, and she didn't want to upset Carole, who had managed only a tight smile when Barbara appeared at the breakfast table. Valerie winked at her as she left the kitchen area and gave her the thumbs-up.

Barbara opened the door to a casually dressed David. He was wearing a light-blue collared shirt and khakis. She was glad she had worn the two-piece turquoise gauzy outfit that Kendra had given her. When she had first received the outfit, she wasn't certain if the style would suit her. But it was one that worked well in the Southwest.

"You look lovely," David said as he gave her a quick peck on the right cheek.

Barbara blushed and stammered, "Thank you." She couldn't believe how nervous she was. He wasn't her first human. In fact, he was her fourth in a little over a year. Number Four! She imagined the other ex-mermaids would discuss that at length. Not at the retreat. Kendra would not allow it, but she had little say in what went on during breaks and in the evenings. Before Carole left on Sunday, Barbara would sit down and have a long chat with her. She didn't want any hurt feelings over all of this.

She followed David to his Jeep. Another Jeep, this one much bigger and more luxurious than Kendra's. He must be doing well as a preacher. Barbara smiled to herself as she recalled an article written about the prosperity gospel that Joel Osteen, Joyce Meyer and the other evangelicals tended to advocate. Not necessarily a bad thing, but many of the religious folk weren't too comfortable with their preachers living lavish lives. Barbara did not begrudge them their wealth. Joel Osteen's telecasts helped her survive those challenging first months on Earth and maintain her equilibrium after the scandal broke out.

"Are you always this quiet?" David asked as he skillfully manoeuvred the Jeep through downtown Sedona.

Barbara was momentarily taken aback as she recalled the same question coming from Stewart as he drove his emerald green Ferrari through the streets of downtown Chicago. She had been on edge the entire weekend and had allowed Stewart to dominate most of the conversations.

"And now you're frowning." David paused.

"I-I'm sorry. Uh, I'm remembering—"

"Someone or something you'd rather forget," David finished.

Barbara laughed. "You must be psychic."

"Not psychic like your friend, Kendra. I'd be in deep trouble if I had to depend upon that ability for a livelihood."

From his tone, Barbara gathered he knew all about Kendra's success. She wondered if he had Googled her as well.

"Henry has highly recommended Cafe Troia and made two reservations for us." He paused. "He thought you might enjoy Italian cuisine."

"Yes, yes I do." Barbara had chatted about some of her favorite dishes on several radio talk shows during the past few months. She decided to test the waters. "How perceptive of Henry. Maybe he has some of those psychic abilities."

David roared with laughter. "Accountant. MBA. He's a poster child for left brainers. Everything has to fit logically or he won't even consider it."

I must fit in Henry's logic scheme. He had Googled, maybe even investigated her, and whatever he found, he must have approved or he wouldn't have sent the flowers, made the lunch reservations, and anointed her as the next Mrs. Ferguson.

Within minutes, they had arrived at the restaurant. Cozy and unpretentious were the first two adjectives came to mind as Barbara's eyes traveled around the large room, taking in the plain décor and widely spaced tables. David was greeted by a server who attended Desertview Church regularly. Barbara and David listened closely as he described the entrées. She selected the *Ossobuco alla Milanese,* veal shank and risotto, while David went with the *Vitella Saltinbocca,* veal scaloppini with prosciutto and mozzarella cheese. The dishes did not disappoint. Barbara had planned to skip dessert, but she quickly changed her mind after watching a couple at the next table *ooh* and *aah* over their cannoli. While eating, their conversation had focused on the delightful food and ambience.

David leaned back in his chair. "So, Ms. Barbara Davies, what brings you to Sedona? Hoping to get away from those brutal Canadian winters?"

"No, I, um . . ." Barbara stuttered. "I'm here to get over a broken engagement." No point holding things back that could implode later. She had had enough experience with that already.

David patted her hand. "If you don't feel comfortable, we don't have to talk about it."

Barbara sensed he didn't want any details. While there's no way he would know anything about the aborted engagement party, he would know about the rest. It wouldn't have taken Henry too long to discover her divorce from the fictitious Carl Davies and her relationship with Graham. She wondered if he had learned about her short-lived fling with Stewart. Thinking back, she didn't recall any pictures taken during that winter weekend in Chicago. Now if Henry had chatted with anyone from Carden, he would know all about the BMW and the scandal that ensued.

David quickly changed the subject. "How long are you staying?"

"I'm here for another three weeks."

He smiled widely. "Good. We'll have lots of time to get to know each other." He lowered his voice. "And maybe I can persuade you to extend your visit."

It wouldn't take much persuading. So far, he had been a charming companion, and she could imagine spending more time with him. Very little awaited her in Canada. The only thing that troubled her was Henry's involvement. She did not appreciate having a voyeur, and while David wouldn't knowingly disclose too many details about their budding relationship, Henry could easily manipulate him.

Barbara longed to know more details about David's reinvention story, but she didn't want to appear too nosy. She decided on another angle. "I'm considering spending the winter. I'm on a leave from my job and could easily complete my book if I had three months of uninterrupted writing time."

"Another book?" David leaned closer. "Am I allowed to ask what it's about?"

"Spectacular second acts," Barbara explained. "I've interviewed over fifty boomer women who've reinvented themselves. I'm hoping to inspire older women who are considering changes in their lives."

"No men?" David joked. "Aren't men allowed to have second acts as well?"

"I hadn't really considered it," Barbara said. "But now that you mention it—"

He shook his finger at her. "So, you Googled me as well?"

They laughed companionably and said nothing for several minutes. David broke the silence. "I don't mind sharing with you, but we . . . I wouldn't be comfortable with any of the details getting out there in print."

Barbara noted the confusion with the pronouns. If Henry were here, she suspected the conversation would end abruptly. Barbara winked. "Not to worry. My publisher has already approved my outline, and I don't think she would be open to any changes. But I'm curious about your move from Texas to Arizona. That is, if you want to talk about it."

He clenched and unclenched his hands. "After Miranda died, I fell apart. I couldn't deal with any of it. The sermons. The congregation. Even God. I was having what is called a crisis of faith and questioned everything I had known for most of life. I had grieved before—grieved my mother most sincerely and many others since becoming a minister. Intellectually, I understood the process, but no amount of understanding was helping. Three months into this crisis, the board called me into a meeting and firmly told me I had to take a sabbatical. I had canceled so many activities and stopped accepting speaking engagements. As for my sermons, well, let's just say lackluster would be the kindest description." He shook his head. "Unbeknownst to me, the board had started interviewing two other pastors who were more than happy to take over until I felt better."

His jaw tightened. "But I knew that I couldn't start again in Dallas. Everywhere I went, I was reminded of Miranda. Her restaurants. Her bookstores. Her walking trails. And of course, the house. So, I resigned my position and let it be known that a congregation was up for grabs. Henry was horrified but said nothing. He let me grieve in peace." He swallowed hard. "When I was ready, he helped me start over. He hired a market research firm to check out several locales and find the one most receptive to an evangelical church." He waved his hand. "And here we are."

Barbara's head was swimming with all these details. She wondered what other locales they had considered but decided not to pry further as she watched him gulp down his coffee and signal the server for another cup. He loosened the collar of his shirt and avoided her glance. She suspected that David had not shared too many details of the past two years with anyone. That is, anyone outside of Henry. And then she realized something else. Henry had also uprooted his life to follow David.

David thanked the server for his coffee and smiled at Barbara. "Which vortex would you like to see this afternoon?"

Reading about the powers of these energy centers had been a welcome distraction after the debacle at Eagle Vision. Barbara had been fascinated by the thought of swirling centers of subtle energy emanating from the surface of the earth. And even more intriguing was the fact that vortex energy was neither electricity nor magnetism.

If a person were sensitive, she could stand at one of these vortexes and let the energy flow in and through her. Super sensitive people could feel that energy as soon as they got out of the Jeep, and the effects lasted several days afterward.

This remarkable energy existed only in Sedona and was the main impetus behind the growing New Age Community that had sprung up in the area. One of the articles had even referred to Sedona as a spiritual Disneyland.

On her own, Barbara intended to visit the Airport Vortex and strengthen her masculine side. In the past, she had never doubted her abilities or felt in any way intimidated, but the coming of Arabella had changed all of that. She needed to build up her confidence again and start taking more risks. This was one goal she had shared with no one, not even Kendra.

Kendra had planned to take them to the Cathedral Rock Vortex on Saturday. Barbara made a mental note to keep that day open and not plan anything with David. That left the Bell Rock and Boynton Canyon Vortexes. Both strengthened the masculine/feminine sides. "How about the Bell Rock Vortex?"

David nodded in approval. "Excellent choice." He paid the server and followed Barbara to the Jeep. In very little time, Barbara caught sight of the vortex's distinctive shape. A handful of vans and Jeeps were in the parking lot and several older couples were pointing toward the vortex. As soon as Barbara got out of the Jeep, she started walking quickly and stopped when she heard David's laugh. "Slow down. The rock isn't going anywhere."

She stopped and waited for him to catch up. They spent the better part of an hour walking and taking pictures. Barbara groaned. "I feel nothing. Absolutely nothing."

"That doesn't surprise me, Barbara. Not at all."

Barbara's eyes widened. "What do you mean?"

He waved his hand. "I'm not disputing the beauty of this place. And all the other vortexes as well. But that's as far as it goes. I think people expect miracles to happen. And maybe it does happen for them. But you and I are different." He winked. "We don't need the vortexes."

But I do. I don't feel balanced at all. Her well-constructed life had been uprooted and she was still trying to get it back together. She managed a smile and tried to hide her disappointment as she followed David to the Jeep.

CHAPTER 25

Barbara arrived at Kendra's as the others were heading toward their rooms. From the glances she received, Barbara gathered she had been the main topic of conversation. Hopefully, none of that talk had spilled into the day's sessions.

Valerie broke away from the group and approached Barbara. Her dark eyes sparkled mischievously. "Are you up for a short walk?"

Barbara followed her outside the door. As they walked in silence, Barbara longed to ask if there had been any gossip, but she didn't want to pressure Valerie into providing details about the day's sessions. While they had connected, Barbara knew that Valerie had strong ties with the others. And they shared a history. These annual retreats had been going on for almost a decade. When they reached the end of the driveway, Valerie broke the silence. "Peck on the cheek or forehead?"

Barbara laughed. "Cheek. How did you—?"

Valerie winked. "I've dated a few men of the cloth."

Barbara's eyes widened. She couldn't imagine irreverent Valerie on a date with a preacher.

"I can watch my mouth for a date or two." Valerie grimaced. "That's really all I could take with those guys. But I'm not you."

Barbara ignored the comment. "I have a favor to ask."

"Shoot."

"I was wondering if I could borrow your car tomorrow." Barbara felt uncomfortable borrowing Kendra's Jeep. She sensed Kendra's disapproval of a relationship with David, and Barbara didn't really want to deal with a stick shift. Valerie's Ford sedan reminded her of her own Corolla, a car she could easily handle.

"Sure, no problem." Valerie frowned. "Why can't he pick you up?"

"Ah, no, I'm . . . I mean, he didn't really ask me out." Barbara reddened. "He mentioned that he would be guest lecturing at Arizona State and I thought I'd—"

"Go out there and see him in action," Valerie finished. "Good idea to take the initiative and show the preacher you're interested. You might get a real kiss out of it."

Both women laughed.

"And while you're out there, do some shopping." Valerie gave her a once-over. "I don't imagine you brought too many date outfits."

One suitcase hastily packed was all she had brought. *Make do with what you have.* The intrusive thought sounded so clear and so forceful that Barbara stopped walking and turned around.

"No ghosts roaming here," Valerie joked. "Kendra won't allow it."

"What about séances and—"

"She's not into any of that stuff with mediums and spirits from the dead. She deals with the here and now and uses the past only as a reference point. Nothing more." She winked at Barbara. "And she doesn't allow any gossip."

Was she that transparent? It was bad enough that Kendra could see right through her. Did Valerie possess that gift as well?

Valerie continued speaking. "The others did make a few comments about Number Four. I caught a bit of envy and awe in their speech. You still have that Bella touch."

Barbara sighed. "I lost those spectacular Bella looks when I gave up my tail."

"Honey, you'll always be the 'It' girl in whatever group you happen to be in. I suspect that's why your sister is so determined to upset your applecart."

After thanking Valerie, Barbara went to her room. She retrieved the tablet and activated it. Lisa738 appeared on the screen with a document in hand. "I have the information, but I don't know where to send it. Do you have access to a printer?"

Barbara shook her head. She was not ready to tell anyone that Annabella had given her five more years of tablet use. At some point, she would share that information with Kendra and Gillian but not today. With the exception of Valerie, Barbara didn't really know the other ex-mermaids very well.

Lisa738 sighed. "I assume you've already obtained the information that's out there via Google." Barbara nodded in agreement and Lisa738 continued, "David was born in Malaysia and did not set foot in the United States until age eighteen. When he arrived at the Texas/Mexico border, Henry was waiting for him."

Barbara's eyes widened. "Hmm . . . So, Henry was there from the start. But how and when did they meet?"

"Two years earlier, Henry had volunteered to help the missionary effort in Nicaragua. He stayed with the Fergusons during that summer and he befriended David. He also promised to help him leave his father's house when he became of age. They corresponded and when David decided to leave, Henry made all the arrangements."

"How bad was his childhood?" Barbara asked.

"His father ruled the household with an iron fist. David and his mother kept the peace as much as possible."

Barbara imagined a younger, more vulnerable David coping with such an authoritative parent. While he probably counted the days until his freedom, it must have been difficult to leave his mother behind. Barbara recalled the delicate features of her fragile beauty. David's departure would have been a devastating blow, one that she never had time to recover from. Barbara remembered reading about an unfortunate accident, but there hadn't been too many details. "How did they die?"

Lisa738 frowned. "A year after David left, an unexplained fire gutted their house. Both died instantly."

"Were the Sadinistas involved?" Reverend Ferguson could have offended someone in the upper echelons of the country's political structure. It didn't sound like he would easily compromise or keep quiet. Not even if his life and that of his wife depended upon it.

Lisa738 shrugged. "Possibly. It could have been faulty wiring."

Or something more sinister. Barbara deliberately brushed that intrusive thought away. She didn't want to think about the anger and acute loneliness that had permeated those four walls once David had left. "What about Henry's family?"

"His father was a minister at a small Baptist church in East Texas. In spite of their less-than-lavish lifestyle, Henry's parents were able to provide him with an Ivy League education. He obtained his undergrad degree at Yale and went on to get an MBA at Harvard. As the youngest of three brothers, he was free to follow his own career path."

The bean counter had chosen to follow a more prosperous path but had still maintained ties to his religious past. "Anything of interest in Henry's life?"

Lisa738 shrugged. "A pretty wife, four children, lots of committees, fundraisers." She flashed a family portrait of the Whitmore family on the screen. Definitely a Texan influence. Lots of big hair and wide-toothed smiles. Henry stood at the back in full patriarch mode while his wife and daughters clustered around him.

"What about that seven-year career gap in David's life?" With the help of Lisa738, Barbara had been able to camouflage her own checkered past. It appeared that David, with Henry's help, had also downplayed his less-than-stellar early years in the United States.

Lisa738 skimmed the document several times. "There were several odd jobs and a few starts at different colleges but nothing significant. It says here . . . He was adapting."

"Excuse me?"

"I'll read it. 'Having lived only in poverty-stricken countries, it took David Ferguson several years to adapt to a rich first-world country. He had never eaten in McDonalds, seen a circus, played team sports, or participated in any of the leisure activities most children take for granted. And he had never attended a public school. His parents had home-schooled him.'"

The culture shock must have been overwhelming. In the end, he had decided to follow in his father's footsteps. But he was a very different kind of preacher. No fire and brimstone, but loving kindness in his sermons and his demeanor.

Barbara sighed. "Anything else of interest?"

Lisa738's eyes twinkled. "He was married to an exotic dancer for twelve days."

"What!" Barbara leaned closer to the tablet.

"During those gap years, he let loose and partied hard. One night, he overindulged and found himself married the following morning. Henry took care of the annulment and paid off the dancer."

Lisa738 held up a grainy, black-and-white picture of David and the woman. While it was hard to make out all the details, it appeared that David was not too thrilled to have his picture taken with the buxom blonde named Pearl Grace. She had a hard look about her and could be anywhere between thirty and forty years of age. One thing was clear. She was much older and more experienced than David.

Barbara squinted at the rustic background. "Where are they?"

"In Mexico," Lisa738 answered. "The morning after their wedding night."

Barbara wondered how many other people Henry had paid off. That juicy tidbit was definitely out there, but only someone as relentless and thorough as Lisa738 would be able to find it. Barbara realized how indebted David was to Henry. He could not have left his father's home or the clutches of the exotic dancer without Henry's help. Barbara was willing to bet that short-lived marriage sobered him up very quickly. "When did he decide on a ministerial career?"

Lisa738 smiled knowingly. "Three weeks after the annulment."

CHAPTER 26

Barbara woke up early the next morning and planned her route to Tempe. Valerie's car had a built-in GPS, but she still didn't trust Earthly technology. Especially after hearing some of the horror stories from the other corporate trainers who experienced GPS power outages and traffic gridlock while driving in downtown Toronto. A small sigh escaped as she recalled the many happy get-togethers with Anne and the others. Before Arabella's arrival, Barbara would think nothing of texting one of her colleagues with an interesting observation or simply to say hello. And make plans to meet for coffee or drinks. But since the suspension, all communication had ceased.

Barbara forced herself to focus on Google Maps. She figured it would be a two-hour drive, maybe even longer, depending on the traffic. David was scheduled to speak at ten o'clock. The lecture would probably run into the noon hour and, if he didn't have other plans, Barbara would treat him to lunch. She wasn't sure of his schedule but figured he would want to eat close to the campus. After researching several nearby establishments, she found herself attracted to The Dhaba that served Indian cuisine and the Desert Roots Kitchen that featured vegan and vegetarian dishes. If neither appealed to David, she would settle for the mesquite-grilled burgers at The Chuck Box.

As she examined the few items hanging in the closet, she reconsidered Valerie's advice. It might not be a bad idea to pick up some blouses. It would certainly give her more options and not put a serious dent in her budget. After checking the expected high temperature for the day, she settled on black dress pants and the red sweater set she had worn on Sunday. And just in case, she grabbed her trench coat. There was a forty-percent chance of an afternoon shower, and she didn't want to be caught unawares.

Barbara had casually mentioned her early departure to Kendra as they were leaving the dinner table. Kendra's expression did not change and before she could comment, Carole announced the board game for the evening. Barbara had been grateful for the reprieve.

Barbara had assumed the others would be chomping at the bit and ready to go out on the town, but they were content to spend their evenings competing with each other over the game of the day. Kendra had planned a day of excursions on Saturday and that seemed to satisfy their need for diversion.

Before leaving for Tempe, Barbara went into the kitchen to grab a quick breakfast. She had planned to pick up a yogurt and apple, but Maria insisted on preparing a proper breakfast. Within minutes, Barbara was seated at the kitchen island, munching on a soft and fluffy cheese omelet.

Maria and Juanita continued with the morning preparations, addressing each other in rapid-fire Spanish. Barbara's eyes misted as she recalled her own facility with all the languages of the Mediterranean, one of the many skills she had been forced to relinquish when she gave up her tail. She wondered if Language Facility was an acceptable Specialist Skill. Not as practical as Financial Acumen but definitely more interesting. She would check with Lisa738 later.

As soon as she finished eating, she sneezed four times.

Maria rushed over. "Are you all right?" She frowned at the empty plate. "Do you have allergies to eggs?"

"No, just seasonal allergies." While Barbara had discussed her Specialist Skills with the other ex-mermaids, she did not feel comfortable sharing this knowledge with

Maria, even though the housekeeper seemed to know all there was to know about the Mediterranean Kingdom. Kendra trusted her completely, and Barbara was certain that Maria was well compensated for her discretion.

Barbara sneezed again. The scent of lavender mingled with roses, gardenias, and several other flowers she could not identify was overpowering. Barbara treated herself to fresh flowers regularly, but she had never experienced this extreme reaction before. She thanked Maria for breakfast and hastily made her way outdoors. Since acquiring Intuition, she had discovered that the smell dissipated as soon as the event occurred or if she went outdoors.

On her way to Valerie's car, she encountered Kendra. The older woman hugged her tightly. "I heard you sneezing. What did you smell?"

"Flowers. Lots of flowers."

"What was the main scent?"

"Lavender."

Kendra raised her eyebrows. "On its own, lavender is usually associated with love and devotion." She paused. "And on the downside, caution, silence, and snakes."

Barbara shuddered at the thought of snakes. "What about the other flowers? I could barely make out the individual flowers."

"Too much of a good thing," Kendra muttered. She hugged Barbara again. "Be careful and don't rush into anything."

Barbara shivered as she made her way to the car. For several minutes, she actually considered canceling her plans for the day. She hadn't promised David, but she didn't feel like participating in the retreat. While she had enjoyed the first two days, she felt uncomfortable sitting with women who had budgeted for this precious time with Kendra.

There were other options. She could shop, sightsee, visit a vortex. But none of them piqued her interest. At least, not today. She took several breaths and centered himself. She would follow the original plan and go to Tempe.

It was a much more stressful drive than she had anticipated, and she was forced to concentrate as she dealt with the stop-and-go traffic on I-17. She breathed a sigh of relief as she neared the university gates. With twenty minutes to spare, she figured it wouldn't take long to find a parking spot and make her way to the lecture hall. But it took much longer and she panicked as she saw 9:57 flashing on the car clock.

Once outside, she was taken aback by the stunning architecture and beautiful foliage. She had visited several smaller universities in Ontario, but none compared to this mammoth institution that housed well over fifty thousand students. She walked briskly, making her way to the Murdock Building. As she entered Room 101, she heard clapping and watched as David made his way to the podium. Thankfully, it was a large auditorium and Barbara had used one of the back entrances. She quickly found a seat and settled in.

The topic, *Finding Your Passion*, was one dear to Barbara's heart and she managed to include it in almost every seminar and workshop. She was enthralled by the presentation, and as she glanced at the rapt faces around her, she realized she wasn't the only one who was inspired by David's talk. His choice of anecdotes was spot on and appealed to the predominantly twenty-something audience. As Barbara's eyes traveled around the auditorium, she caught glimpses of several older gentlemen who were also listening intently and nodding as David spoke.

As soon as the Q & A period started, hands went up all around Barbara. Two young women with microphones sprinted around the hall selecting students at random. Most of the questions centered on following your passion and career selection. David skillfully addressed all the questions, often meeting with applause.

"Last question," one of the female runners shouted as she approached a male student.

"I'm wondering about your experience with gap years. From what I've read, it sounds like you had seven of them. What's up with that, Rev?"

David did not miss a beat. He joined in the laughter and waited for the audience members to settle down. "What can I say? I'm a slow learner and needed that time to evolve." He waved his hands toward the audience. "From what I've heard this morning, I gather that most of you are more focused than I ever was. And I applaud you for it. In this economy, you can't afford to take too many gap years."

The student persisted, "But what did you do during that time?"

Henry rose and approached the podium. "I think Reverend Ferguson has addressed your first question, young man. Which, if I recall correctly, was the last question. I would invite anyone who didn't get a chance to ask questions to email us."

Smooth, Barbara thought. Henry had put the interloper in his place and managed to convey that David was open to all questions via email. Questions that would be screened by Henry and the other gatekeepers who reported to him.

When David sat down, a woman approached the podium and thanked David for taking time out of his busy schedule to speak with students. Barbara waited until most of the students left before making her way to the front of the auditorium. David saw her first. His eyes lighted up and he started walking toward Barbara. The older gentleman, with whom he had been speaking, frowned and shook his head. David must have left in the middle of the conversation without excusing himself.

David hugged her and whispered, "What a surprise! I'm so glad to see you here."

"I love listening to you speak," Barbara said. "How about lunch?"

"You can join us. We're going to—"

Henry harrumphed. "Good morning, Barbara. This is a surprise." His eyes traveled around the auditorium. "Are you here with Ms. Adams?"

"No, I decided to play hooky and miss another day of the retreat."

"You drove here by yourself?" Henry narrowed his eyes. "I could have picked you up or asked my wife to attend this lecture. There was no need for you to drive alone. Especially on the I-17 during the morning rush hour."

Barbara smiled. "I do a lot of driving in Ontario and most of it during rush hour." She had definitely upset Henry's plans for the day. She suspected that he was having second thoughts about her suitability as the next Mrs. Ferguson. He might have been able to manipulate Miranda, but Barbara was not willing to be his next puppet.

The older gentleman approached. "Gentlemen, I hate to interrupt, but if we're going to have lunch, we'd better get a move on. I have another meeting at one-thirty."

Barbara surmised that neither Henry nor the older gentleman were too keen on her attendance. "It sounds like you're planning a business lunch. I'll take a rain check for another day." She winked at David.

Henry relaxed and favored her with a smile. "That would be best. How about Nora and I treat you to lunch tomorrow at our place? I will pick you up at eleven." Without waiting for her response, he walked away. David and the other gentleman followed.

In the end, she had been skillfully manipulated by a master in the art and was left fuming. She really didn't want to spend tomorrow afternoon with Henry and his wife, who may not be too thrilled with the impromptu invitation. As Barbara walked toward the parking lot, she considered her other options for the afternoon. She could treat herself to a shopping spree in Tempe or Phoenix, but she didn't enjoy shopping on her own. If she waited until Saturday, she could shop with Valerie and the others at Arizona Mills. From the evening conversations, she gathered that was one of the high points of their annual visit. And, deep down, Barbara knew that she could easily overspend when she was bored or agitated. Thankfully, that hadn't happened too often, but it was definitely an issue to consider.

In the end, her grumbling stomach made the decision. Five hours had passed without a snack or beverage and she didn't feel like driving too far without food in her stomach. She headed toward the Desert Roots Kitchen where she had the large Hummus Plate. It was close to two o'clock when she finally left the restaurant, feeling more calm and centered. The waitress had advised against dawdling too long in Tempe if she wanted to avoid the congestion that would soon overtake the route. The weather had warmed up considerably and Barbara kept her window open as she drove back to Sedona.

CHAPTER 27

Valerie was sitting on a lounger enjoying her martini. "Just in time," she called out as Barbara got out of the car. She waved her hand toward the pitcher. "Madam, your martini awaits."

Barbara was enjoying these afternoon chats with Valerie and would be sorry to see the younger woman leave on Sunday. Albuquerque was not that far from Sedona. Five hours or so, Barbara estimated. A leisurely weekend drive if she decided to stay in Arizona, and if Valerie was willing to continue the friendship.

Barbara glanced at her watch and was surprised to see that it was getting close to five o'clock. The other ex-mermaids were probably napping or getting ready for dinner at six. How kind of Valerie to give up her free time. Barbara poured herself a martini and took a generous gulp. While drinking, her eyes traveled around the beautifully maintained English gardens. It would be so easy to stay here indefinitely, enjoying all of this bounty. All of Kendra's bounty, that is. But Barbara would not take advantage of her. At the end of the month, or before, she would make a final decision regarding her stay in Arizona.

While Henry's manipulative behavior was annoying, Barbara was interested in pursuing a relationship with David. He definitely appealed to her spiritual side, something that neither Graham nor Stewart would ever have satisfied. While she hadn't discussed spirituality with Stewart, she suspected that religion did not play a large part in his life. As for Graham, he still associated Catholicism with his wife's death, something that would probably never change. Dear Graham. Teaching and toiling in Vermont. Would he ever forgive her? And if he did, would she go back to him? That last question startled her. A week ago, she would not have even considered that possibility.

"You're frowning again," Valerie said. "If you're not careful, you'll be spending time and money in a cosmetic surgeon's office."

"Never, never—" Barbara started to say and then realized that most of the ex-mermaids in her circle had been under the knife, so to speak. And while Valerie hadn't undergone major surgery, she freely admitted to Botox and fillers.

Valerie patted the lounger. "Come sit down and tell me all about lunch with the preacher."

Barbara gave Valerie a quick summary of the day's events. Valerie's eyes narrowed. "You'll have to get Henry out of the picture. Kindly but firmly tell him to mind his own business."

"Not so easy to do," Barbara muttered.

"Henry isn't David's father. He's one of the gatekeepers, easily expendable." Valerie's voice rose. "David doesn't owe him anything beyond that hefty salary."

"Henry and his wife left Texas and relocated to Arizona—"

"He probably made a tidy profit on his Texas home. Trust me, Henry benefited in many ways by this move, and he'll continue to benefit as long as he stays hitched to David's star." Valerie poked Barbara. "Nothing wrong with making an extra buck but that doesn't give him the right to interfere or make decisions about David's relationships."

Barbara smiled tightly but said nothing. With Valerie, she had skimmed over the details about David's past, steering clear of any mention of Pearl Grace. David was beholden to Henry and would always keep him close by. And Henry would not leave of his own accord. If she continued with this relationship, she would have to deal with Henry's presence.

Wait and see. The intrusive thought was almost a whisper. Good advice, Barbara thought as she sipped her martini. Now all she had to do was steer the conversation in a different direction.

"So, what are you wearing tomorrow?" Valerie asked.

"My turquoise outfit. It's fresh and—"

"He's already seen it," Valerie finished as she poured herself another martini. "You should have gone shopping while you were in Tempe. You were minutes away from Arizona Mills." She sat up and snapped her fingers. "I've got the perfect church dress for you. Complete with matching purse, gloves, and—"

Barbara laughed. "You've got to be kidding?" While she wasn't sure what constituted a "church dress" she doubted very much that Valerie would have packed such an outfit.

"When Carole went on and on about David in her emails, I figured we'd all get invitations to some kind of church event, so I packed one." Valerie winked. "My first man was a staunch Baptist, so I know all about proper church wear."

Barbara winced at the mention of Carole obsessing over David. There had been a noticeable distancing since the flowers had arrived, but she couldn't focus on that now. She gave Valerie's tall, slim figure a once-over. "I doubt that it would fit."

"Honey, you're getting pretty close to skin and bones yourself." She glanced critically at Barbara's legs. "It'll probably hit mid-calf which is okay, considering where you're going."

Barbara followed the younger woman inside and upstairs to her bedroom. Valerie went directly to the closet and pulled out a floral lilac-colored outfit. A pretty pattern but not one that Barbara would have chosen. It reminded her of Victorian era tablecloths and older ladies at afternoon teas. After throwing the dress on the bed, Valerie scooped up a sea of lilac—clutch purse, shoes, gloves—and a large white straw hat with a lilac ribbon. After assembling all the pieces on the bed, Valerie raised her arms. "Ta-da!"

"I cannot believe that you would even consider—"

Valerie's eyes twinkled, "Oh, yes I would. I love costumes and that's all this is. A costume to please the preacher and his sidekick." She clapped her hands. "Let's get started."

CHAPTER 28

Barbara woke up to the sun streaming in through the windows. As her eyes adjusted to the daylight, she groaned at the sight of the lilac costume. It had fit well, perhaps too well, and showed off her curves a bit more than she was used to, but Valerie was ecstatic and assured her that she would wow both David and Henry.

Another groan escaped at the thought of Henry. While she appreciated the invitation, she had no intention of spending the afternoon with the Whitmores. Somehow, she would get time alone with David. Trying to come up with a viable suggestion that would not interest Henry and Nora had kept her awake for most of the night. She intended to visit the other three vortexes, but she didn't think that David was that keen on accompanying her. Hopefully, something would come to her later.

In the meantime, she had three hours to kill before lunch. After a quick shower, she dressed in her jeans and a sweatshirt and went downstairs to the kitchen. On the way, she encountered a groggy Carole, who nodded in Barbara's direction.

Barbara was glad that none of the others had come down yet. It would give her a chance to talk with Carole and settle the David issue once and for all.

Carole smiled without humor. "Any plans for the day?"

"I'm having lunch with David at Henry's house."

"You're making progress. If Henry invited—"

Barbara interrupted her. "We need to clear the air

regarding David. I don't want you to think that I had designs on him and tried to take him away—"

Carole leaned over and squeezed her arm. "Honey, it was just a crush."

"But you purposely came here to—"

Carole held up her hand. "I came here for the retreat. That's something I've been doing for the past ten years and will probably continue doing for several more years. End of story." She smiled at Maria, who brought over two plates of crepes.

While Barbara wasn't convinced, she realized the topic was no longer on the table. Carole might share her true feelings with the others, but Barbara would not be privy to them. Before Barbara could say anything more, Laura and Tamara arrived. The conversation assumed a lighter tone and no one else brought up David.

When Barbara finished eating, she excused herself and went back upstairs. She set her timer for sixty minutes and took out her laptop. She had come up with an idea for an introduction to her book. And Barbara had every intention of honoring the arrival of the muse that had disappeared after the eventful supper. As thoughts of Arabella flooded her mind, Barbara turned her attention to the notes she had jotted down during David's lecture. After rereading the notes and recalling the intensity in David's voice, she started writing an essay entitled *Resurrecting Passion*. When the timer rang, she was pleased to discover that she had written over two thousand words.

She walked over and picked up the lilac dress. If she thought of it as a costume, it would be easier to get through the day. But wouldn't that set up false expectations? Would David and Henry—yes, Henry was in the picture and would probably stay there—want her to always dress that way?

It didn't take long to get dressed, apply her makeup, and do her hair. As she surveyed herself in the full-length mirror, she frowned at the demure church lady. *That's* what she had become. And she wasn't sure if she liked this role or if she was even suited to it. As she picked up the ridiculously small clutch, she sneezed several times. Yesterday's overwhelming scent had returned, and this time the roses and lavender dominated. She glanced at her watch and figured she had fifteen minutes before Henry arrived. Enough time to step outdoors and allow the scent to dissipate.

As Barbara made her way downstairs, she heard Henry's voice. And Kendra's. While she couldn't make out the entire conversation, she heard Henry mention something about continuing the conversation later in the day. He had once again foiled her plans for the afternoon. Barbara inwardly groaned. She wouldn't be getting any one-on-one time with David, and Kendra's afternoon would also be disrupted.

"My dear, Barbara. You are a vision of loveliness." Henry approached and took her hand. "If only Mrs. Ferguson were alive to see you today. She would be simply overcome as . . . as I am overcome."

It took several seconds for the name to register. Henry was referring to the first Mrs. Ferguson, David's mother. Barbara managed a smile and reluctantly made eye contact with Henry. A Duchenne smile lit up his face, and to her surprise, he hugged her tightly and gave her a quick peck on the cheek.

Barbara noticed the other ex-mermaids standing near Kendra. All except Valerie, who would hear about this later and put her own spin on events. As Barbara and Henry walked toward the door, a breathless voice rang out. "Miss Barbara! Miss Barbara! Your hat. You forgot your hat."

The minx! Barbara plastered a smile on her face as Valerie walked quickly toward her. Her dark eyes twinkled mischievously as she handed the hat to Barbara.

Henry winked at Valerie. "I'll make sure we spend some time outdoors." He smiled at Kendra. "We'll be back by four. Thank you so much for inviting us to tea. I know that Nora will be over the moon."

So, that's what the earlier conversation had been about. He had managed to somehow wrangle an invitation from Kendra, who was smiling graciously and wishing them a happy day. Barbara followed Henry outside and was grateful for the fresh air that chased away the annoying scent. Hopefully, that would be the end of it for today.

Henry excused himself and walked over to the other side of the verandah, well out of earshot. He took out his cell phone and placed a quick call. Less than a minute in length, the conversation put him in an even better mood. There was a skip in his step as he walked over to a silver-colored Cadillac Escalade.

"How lovely," Barbara said as she stroked the soft leather seats. "It feels like I'm floating on a cloud."

"And they're heated as well," Henry said. "Though, I doubt we'll need that today." He smiled at the hat sitting on Barbara's lap. "It'll be a special treat to see you in that hat, and I'll persuade Nora to wear one of hers. We'll take pictures."

Barbara was surprised at how young and carefree he sounded. In his chinos and denim shirt, he seemed much more approachable. Of course, the church outfit had scored and put him in such a good mood. It was bit disconcerting just how accurately Valerie had pegged him. Barbara wondered about David's reaction and secretly hoped he would be amused rather than impressed. She smiled at Henry. "Where's David?"

"He had an emergency call this morning."

"Nothing serious, I hope." While she was comfortable with the relaxed Henry, she didn't want to spend the day without David.

"He should be back soon." Henry cleared his throat.

"I'm glad we have this time alone, Barbara. There are a few things you need to know about David."

You mean about Pearl Grace and the wild years. The intrusive thought sounded so loud. Had she blurted it out? One glance at Henry convinced her she had not.

Henry continued, "When Miranda died two years ago, David was a mess. He couldn't cope. He withdrew from everyone and everything involved with the ministry. We gave him space and slowly he came back to us. You're the first woman he's shown an interest in and, well, I'm glad . . . glad it's you and not one of those Jezebels who throw themselves at him." He shuddered. "You wouldn't believe the notes and emails these women send. The late-night phone calls. One woman even tried to befriend Nora with that sole purpose in mind. No shame. No shame at all." His voice had risen and Barbara caught glimpses of an angry flush staining his cheeks.

For a while, no one spoke. Henry muttered something unintelligible when a car passed him. His hands tightened around the leather-wrapped steering wheel and it looked like he was white-knuckling it. It wasn't even rush hour and the traffic flow on the secondary highway was manageable. Not certain how to respond, Barbara focused on the scenery.

CHAPTER 29

Barbara had no idea where they were, and she didn't think it wise to question Henry. He had calmed down considerably since his tirade about the Jezebels, but he still exuded tension. She gathered from several road signs that they were about sixty miles away from Phoenix. And Prescott was somewhere to the west of their present whereabouts. Her maps were in the large tote she had abandoned in favor of the child-sized clutch. All to complete the ideal church lady image that Valerie had imposed upon her. Right now, the one hundred percent polyester costume was sticking to her. The car thermometer read seventy-three degrees, but it was much warmer than that. She longed to turn on the air conditioning but didn't feel comfortable doing so without Henry's permission.

Henry started slowing down. They had arrived. As soon as he parked the SUV, the front door opened and a small, slim woman emerged. Cute and cuddly were two adjectives that immediately came to mind as Barbara's eyes traveled over Nora's small frame and took in the bouffant blond hairdo, cornflower blue eyes and upturned nose. Barbara couldn't help smiling at her outfit. She was wearing an aqua print dress similar in style to her own lilac costume. Maybe a coincidence but probably not as Barbara recalled the short call that Henry had placed. This must be one of his directives.

Nora approached and hugged Barbara. "I'm so glad to meet you. I feel like I know you already."

"I feel the same way," Barbara replied truthfully. Nora reminded her of Lisa738. And with a pang Barbara realized they had not spoken since Monday. With the election preparations in full swing, all the Numbers Mermaids had been asked to put in extra hours. Barbara had decided not to contact Lisa738 until Saturday evening.

Henry laughed. "I knew you two would hit it off right away. This was meant to be."

Nora nodded happily and before anyone could respond, the sliding doors opened and David emerged. He raised his eyebrows as he glanced from one woman to the other. His eyes were brimming with mirth and Barbara was certain he would explode with laughter once they were alone. The costume had not been necessary.

As Nora took her on a tour of the house, Barbara could see little evidence of Henry. The house was all Nora with its Country Farmhouse décor. And when they entered the large eat-in kitchen with saffron-colored walls and glass-fronted cabinets, an impressive table awaited them. Everything from the succulent leg of lamb roast to the grilled tomatoes and broiled eggplant were cooked to perfection.

Henry dominated the conversation, intent on learning more about Barbara's career. "But what exactly does your job entail?"

"I'm a corporate trainer," Barbara explained. "I provide in-service mainly for employees at large firms."

Henry raised an eyebrow. "What type of in-service?"

Barbara managed a tight smile. He seemed a bit too interested in her job. Had he poked around and learned about her suspension? She cleared her mind and tried to recall her schedule during the first two weeks of the month. "Some of my presentations involve Dealing with Difficult People, Assertive Communication, and Managing Job Stress. A popular one is Building Confidence, Competence and Credibility."

Henry smiled approvingly. "I like the sound of all of

them, especially the last one. Would you consider sharing your gifts while you're here? You could—"

David frowned at Henry. "Barbara is taking a break from her job. And she's working on her next book. I don't think we should be asking her to take time away from that."

As the two men exchanged glances, Barbara could feel the tension rise in the room. She really should say something. She could offer to facilitate one workshop but knowing Henry, he would not be satisfied with only one offering. Before long, she would be booked solid and offering her services at no cost. Of that, she was certain. "Sharing your gifts" was a nice way of asking for a freebie.

"And now for dessert," Nora said as she stood. "I'll make some tea and—"

Henry waved his hand. "Not for me, dear. David and I have to go over some accounts, so we shall leave you two lovely ladies to your own amusements."

David rose and followed Henry to his den.

Once the men were out of earshot, Nora giggled. "I knew they'd go as soon as I mentioned dessert."

What an odd comment, Barbara thought. But Nora was more attuned to the moods of her husband and knew how to smooth over those awkward moments. Barbara smiled brightly. "They don't eat dessert?"

"Oh, they love their pies, puddings, and cakes, but that's not what I planned for today."

Barbara was intrigued. While Nora Whitmore went along with many of her husband's requests, she did have a mind of her own when it came to her domain. Before Barbara could comment, Nora left the room and returned a few seconds later with a large tray. Her cheeks were flushed and there was a hint of animation in her eyes. She removed the plastic covering and placed the tray on the kitchen counter.

Barbara was impressed by the sea of pink, cream, and chocolate that unfolded before her. Designer cupcakes.

Those miniature creations that could easily derail the most disciplined of dieters. "Oh, Nora, you shouldn't have, but I'm glad you did." Barbara carefully examined each cupcake and finally decided to try the chocolate cupcake topped with a frothy hazelnut butter cream. She smiled as she savored the taste. "Mmm. Simply exquisite."

"Chocolate Haze. That's one of my favorites," Nora said as she helped herself to the lemony-looking cupcake.

"Tell me about the others." Barbara pointed toward the remaining cupcakes on the tray.

"The first on the left is called Nostalgia. It's a classic vanilla cake topped with creamy vanilla frosting. Next to it is Cuppa-Sunshine—a lemony cupcake topped with a citrus butter cream. Love Spell is vanilla and chocolate marbled together and topped with a semi-sweet chocolate ganache. The last one is Cupcake Bling, a party favorite. It's a chocolate cake with strawberry buttercream rolled in pink rock candy."

"You came up with all of this on your own?" Barbara thought of her Specialist Skill in Cuisine that allowed her to hold her own with the likes of Rachael Ray, Martha Stewart, and Nigella Lawson. Nora Whitmore also belonged to that elite group. "You are so creative, Nora."

Nora sighed. "It's nice to hear that I am still able to impress someone."

"I'm willing to bet that you impress a lot of people." Barbara caught the tinges of sadness in Nora's voice. After three decades of marriage, Henry probably took her for granted, not realizing what a gem he had in his wife. And for reasons unknown, Nora had allowed that to happen. Barbara was curious but did not want to pry into those reasons. Her eyes traveled back to the tray. "I really shouldn't—"

"Go on," Nora said. "I will if you will."

They laughed companionably and both picked up another cupcake. Barbara was pleased with her second choice of

Nostalgia and she smiled approvingly at Nora's choice of Chocolate Haze. As Barbara sipped her tea, she felt herself slipping into a safe cocoon of comfort. Nora had created a cozy world for herself, out here in the Arizona outback. Barbara had asked several times but no one had been able to tell her exactly where the Whitmore house was located. All she had been able to deduce was that it was east of Prescott and north of Phoenix.

CHAPTER 30

Barbara had braced herself for a long afternoon, but to her surprise, the time passed quickly. After finishing their cupcakes, the conversation gravitated toward Nora's bread-making machine. Before Barbara could comment, she found herself wrapped in an apron and preparing the ingredients for a loaf of sweet bread. In very little time—Barbara figured an hour or so—a perfect honey and buttermilk loaf emerged.

While waiting, Nora chatted about her family and Nicaragua. Barbara was surprised at how much of the conversation focused on the three months Nora had spent in one of the poorest countries in the Western Hemisphere. As Barbara glanced through the three scrapbooks, she saw a very different Nora and Henry. Younger in appearance and spirit, they looked ready to take on any challenge. And that optimism was evident in all the pictures.

"It was the best time of my life," Nora said wistfully. "I could have stayed there forever."

Barbara's eyes widened at the thought of delicate Nora and fastidious Henry settling in a third-world country with economic and political problems.

Nora laughed. "I know. I know. We may not look too adventurous now, but back then nothing fazed us. And those three months were challenging ones. There were supposedly two seasons—wet and dry, but I quickly discovered there were really three seasons: wet, dry, and dusty, which occurred in sequence every three hours. The water and electricity were on for only part of the day." An excited gleam appeared in her eyes. "I experienced my first hurricane there. Major flooding and mudslides. Nicaragua kept us on our toes."

The contrast between Nora's beautifully decorated house and the shacks and cinderblock structures in the album couldn't be more striking, but Nora's heart was still in Nicaragua. Almost forty years had passed and Nora's passion had not abated. And from the pictures, it looked like Henry had also shared that enthusiasm.

"You're probably wondering why we left." Nora's eyes grew moist. "In the end, Henry and I just couldn't imagine working under Reverend Ferguson. He oversaw most of the missions in the country and had very strong opinions on almost every topic. He tried our patience dearly during those three months, but we maintained our cheerfulness and managed to avoid any major rows. Had we stayed longer, Henry would have butted heads with him, and the situation would have become untenable." She let out a quick breath and shook her head, as though shaking off the emotions rising up inside her. "We had a hard time leaving David. He had become attached to Henry and spent a lot of that summer with us. We were his only diversion."

Barbara continued to look at the picture. "How old were you?"

"I was twenty-one and Henry was twenty-two." She sighed. "David was sixteen and miserable. It tore at our hearts to leave and abandon our ministries."

"You could have gone to another country. Lots of souls to save around the world."

Nora's eyes glistened with tears. "We had to save David."

Even though Barbara had heard some of the details from Lisa738, she was moved by Nora's account and felt even more protective of David. Those years he spent waiting for his eighteenth birthday must have been excruciating ones. Nora blew her nose and started to put away the scrapbooks.

The aroma of freshly baked bread traveled throughout the house and within minutes David and Henry were in the kitchen. In spite of Nora's admonishments about saving room for tea and dinner, the men treated themselves to two slices of bread each. Nora and Barbara shared one slice. As Barbara contemplated the machine, she decided that it would not be a good purchase. She would not be able to resist using it regularly and the pounds would creep up. But if she stayed here in Arizona, she could easily satisfy her bread-making urge by visiting Nora. As Barbara's eyes traveled around the room, she took in the relaxed mood that was due mainly to Nora's efforts. While her marriage may have its challenging moments, they didn't seem to linger.

Barbara sneezed. Five sneezes in succession.

Everyone stopped speaking. Nora was at her side immediately. "What can I get you? Benadryl? Reactin? Neocitran?"

Barbara frowned as she breathed in the odor of burnt coffee beans. A familiar smell that she had associated with Arabella. But Arabella was thousands of miles away wreaking havoc in other people's lives. *What was her intuition trying to tell her?* Barbara forced herself to smile. "No, no, I'm fine. Just fighting some allergies."

Nora pointed to the bread. "I wonder if you're allergic to gluten."

"I don't know." Barbara figured if she had to have an allergy it might as well be gluten. "I'll have to get that checked out."

Nora walked over to a small desk in the corner and pulled out a large black binder. She flipped through the pages quickly. "I know an allergist in Phoenix who could take you tomorrow, even today."

Henry pointed to his watch. "Not now, honey. It's already past three. We need to get going if we're going to make tea at four o'clock. I don't imagine Ms. Adams has too much free time with all those women underfoot." He frowned. "What do they do all day?"

Barbara caught glimpses of exchanged smiles between David and Nora. Henry would certainly be out of his element at a retreat of any kind. Barbara addressed Henry. "The days are jam-packed with activities and exercises. It's similar to what I do with my presentations except there are shared meals and sleepovers."

"What time is supper?" Nora asked. "We don't want to overstay our welcome and keep Ms. Adams from her duties as hostess."

"We eat at six, but Kendra doesn't handle any of that. Maria and Juanita prepare all the meals and snacks."

Henry spoke forcefully. "Ladies, you have exactly five minutes to get yourselves ready." He headed outdoors while David saluted him and winked in our direction. Nora and David had his number down pat and went along with his requests. Barbara shrugged and followed suit as Nora pointed her in the direction of the powder room.

Once outside, Barbara breathed easily through her nostrils. The burnt coffee bean's odor was gone and hopefully nothing too earth-shattering would occur in the Arizona outback.

Barbara had hoped to ride in David's Jeep, but for some reason, they all piled up in Henry's SUV. The two men sat in the front and Barbara shared the back seat with Nora and a silver tray filled with cupcakes. Nora had mentioned bringing some homemade jams and preserves, but Barbara had assured her the cupcakes would be more than enough. As Henry drove, Nora kept glancing at the cupcakes and smiling. She was secretly proud of them and Barbara knew that Kendra and the other ex-mermaids would *ooh* and *aah* over them. Nora needed those extra doses of validation. *You can help her with that.* Barbara smiled as she acknowledged the intrusive thought.

A honking and fast-moving black vehicle forced Henry to slow down and drive on the shoulder. "What the hell?" He brought the SUV to a stop and pulled out his cell phone.

"Henry, no!" Nora cried out.

"It's probably some kids on a joy ride," David said. "Let it go."

"I don't think so," Henry muttered. "Those kids need to be taught a lesson. A lesson they can easily afford if they're driving a BMW."

Barbara's heart skipped several beats. *A black BMW here in the Arizona outback. Could this be what the burnt coffee smell was all about?*

"Hello, Steve. Henry Whitmore calling. Uh . . . yes, fine . . . well, not so fine after a bunch of hooligans in a fancy black BMW drove me off the road." There was a short pause and Henry spoke again. "I think one of your boys needs to let these jokers know what they can't get away with in Arizona." Another pause. "Looks like a rental. They're headed north on 179 toward Sedona. About twenty miles out, I'd say." Henry turned toward David who only nodded. "Thanks, Chief. Looking forward to our golf game next Tuesday."

Barbara tried to make eye contact, but Nora kept her head down and refused to meet her glance. Barbara gathered it was not the first time that Henry had called the police chief with his complaints.

Henry eased the Jeep back on the road. For the next several miles, no one spoke. David focused on the outside scenery while Nora kept her gaze straight ahead. Her lips tightened as she rummaged through her purse and pulled out a large pair of sunglasses. The earlier mood had been shattered.

"Damnation!" Henry shouted. "What's wrong with these people?"

The black BMW was driving erratically on the shoulder

and the road, weaving back and forth. The driver was definitely under some influence. Drugs. Alcohol. Or maybe just joy riding.

"I have a good mind to block them and—"

"No," David said firmly. "They're obviously high and not behaving too logically. If you block them, they will retaliate."

"Let's go home," Nora said quietly. She turned to Barbara. "You can have supper with us, and I'll drive you back later this evening."

Henry's eyebrows furrowed in the rearview mirror. "I will not give them the satisfaction of driving me off this road." He picked up speed and passed using the left lane. Within minutes, the BMW was tailgating them.

"Henry, pull to the side and let them pass," Nora pleaded. "It's not worth it."

David made eye contact with Henry but said nothing.

After a few more minutes of tailgating, Henry groaned and finally let the BMW pass.

"A woman is driving," Nora said.

"Women drivers," Henry muttered, "They shouldn't be allowed. Did you see that?" His voice rose. "She gave me the finger."

"That's the least of it," Barbara muttered.

"Excuse me!" Henry shouted as he glanced in the rearview mirror.

"It could have been much worse," Barbara explained. "She could have rammed into your vehicle and caused all sorts of damage."

"Barbara's right," Nora said. "We've been spared an accident." She leaned over and squeezed Barbara's arm.

Barbara managed a smile but inwardly she was seething. How dare this man put all of them in harm's way? He had alerted the police to possible danger on the road. Why couldn't he leave it at that? And why was David saying nothing? He hadn't even turned around to reassure her. *This is how it will be.* Barbara countered with her own unspoken thought. *Do I really need, or even want, these men in my life?* While she had no control over Henry's moods, she could control her reactions to him. And she could limit her encounters with him even if that meant seeing less of David.

A police cruiser with its lights flashing whizzed right by them.

"About time," Henry said. He drove in silence the rest of the way. As Henry neared Kendra's house, Barbara heard Nora's sharp intake of breath. The police cruiser had pulled up to Kendra's driveway. A man and woman were standing near the black BMW, pointing toward the house. As if on cue, Kendra and the ex-mermaids appeared on the verandah.

Henry parked with a flourish right next to the police cruiser. Before anyone could say anything, he turned off the ignition and raced toward the policeman. Barbara heard a groan from the front seat and a sigh from Nora. "I hope they're not Kendra's friends," Nora said.

"Probably clients or wannabe clients," David said. "Lost souls looking for direction."

"She's beautiful," Nora said softly.

Barbara followed Nora's gaze and gasped. Arabella, in a heated argument with Henry.

CHAPTER 31

"Let's get this over with," David muttered as he unhooked his seatbelt.

Another sigh escaped from Nora. "Should I leave the cupcakes for later or—?"

"Take them out now," David said. "I think everyone could use the distraction."

Barbara slowly unhooked her own belt and followed Nora and David out of the SUV. Of all the possible mishaps that could have occurred today, meeting up with Arabella wasn't even on her radar. While the burnt coffee beans should have alerted her to that possibility, she hadn't even considered it. And now she must prepare herself for the worst.

Strangely enough, she didn't feel the same agitation she had experienced during her previous encounters with Arabella. An eerie calmness had descended upon her, and she found herself more curious than upset by her twin sister's unexpected arrival.

David slammed the door purposefully while Nora made her way to the front porch. Each of the ex-mermaids took a cupcake and started gushing over them. Arabella and Henry were momentarily distracted by the activity. David and the officer smiled at each other. Stewart's eyes widened, but he said nothing.

He's surprised to see me here. Could this be a coincidence? But knowing Arabella it was not. Somehow, her conniving twin sister had learned of Barbara's whereabouts and talked Stewart into taking a holiday in Arizona. And from what

Paul and Gillian had told her, the man was so besotted with Arabella that he indulged every whim. But that was before the flings, indiscretions, or Barbara wasn't really sure what to call all that bad behavior.

Henry was the first to break the silence. "Officer, I insist that you give this . . . this woman a ticket. And test her blood-alcohol level. She's obviously impaired." He glared at Stewart. "And as for you, I suggest you keep a tighter rein on your daughter. She shouldn't be driving."

Arabella laughed. "He's my husband, Grandpa. And no one tells me what I should be doing or not doing, least of all you." She shook her long tresses vigorously as she twirled on one foot, exposing a substantial amount of midriff. Dressed in head-to-toe black, her tight cropped top and ripped jeans clung to every curve. As her high-pitched laugh increased in volume, she started blowing kisses at Stewart, David, and Henry. While Stewart averted his glance and Henry's eyes narrowed in disgust, David appeared amused by the whole affair. A smile played on his lips as he gave Arabella a once-over.

He's intrigued. And curious. While Arabella looked nothing like Pearl Grace, she did exude those bad-girl vibes. *And that's what he wants.* Barbara's thoughts flashed back to the conversation with Henry. The Jezebels must have felt encouraged. That's why they pursued David so relentlessly.

Henry spoke directly to the officer while waving his hand toward David and Barbara. "My friends can support my testimony. She drove erratically the entire time—"

Arabella smirked as she made eye contact with Barbara. "Well, well if it isn't my long-lost sister, Barbara." Her eyes traveled toward David. "Didn't take you long to find Number Four." She winked. "And this one is a cutie!"

"Your sister!" Henry roared as he glared at Barbara. "Do you know this Jezebel?"

Nora handed the tray to Carole and raced down the steps.

She grabbed Henry's arm. "Honey, please don't get yourself riled up. Let's just get into the car and go home. Remember what the doctor said about your blood pressure—"

Henry let out his breath in disgust. "I'm not leaving until Barbara answers my question. And I would also like to know what the Jezebel meant by Number Four."

"I can help you with all of that." Arabella giggled. "You see, Barbara and I are mermaid sisters." She pointed toward Kendra and the other ex-mermaids. "And they're mermaids, as well. We all belong to the Mediterranean tribe—"

The officer chuckled and put away his book. "Folks, let's call this a day." He spoke directly to Kendra. "Ms. Adams, I leave everyone here in your very capable hands. I'm sure you can sort it out."

Henry followed the officer to his car. "Officer, I insist that you—"

"Mr. Whitmore, I have decided to walk away from this situation." The officer nodded in David's direction. "Reverend."

Henry shouted, "I will take this up with the Chief."

"Go right ahead," the officer said as he got into the cruiser and drove away.

"Unbelievable!" Henry yelled. "After all the support we've given the local police force, you think we could get some justice." He gestured toward Arabella, who had moved further away from him. "I can smell the marijuana from here. And I wouldn't be surprised if she's on cocaine—"

"Nothing wrong with smoking a bit of pot and that's all I'm smoking. Last time, I checked, Grandpa, pot's legal." She began to walk toward him but stumbled over a rock and would have fallen had Stewart not caught her.

Henry approached, waving his finger menacingly in Arabella's face. "Don't tell me what's legal and what's not, Missy. You're so high you can't even walk straight. If it were up to me—"

David approached Henry and whispered something in his ear as he stroked the older man's arm. Henry took several deep breaths, nodding as David continued to whisper in his ear. The men were standing very close to each other, engrossed in an intense conversation, oblivious to everyone around them.

Arabella's eyes widened as she continued to study the two men. She released another high-pitched laugh as she spoke directly to Barbara. "Didn't know you were into threesomes with the lavender crowd."

A strangled sob escaped from Nora, who ran toward the SUV. Henry ran after her while David stood frozen, his face devoid of all color. He started to speak and then changed his mind as he made his way to the van.

No one spoke until the SUV left the premises.

Kendra approached Arabella and Stewart. After a quiet conversation, Arabella lowered her head and allowed herself to be accompanied into the house. The ex-mermaids waited until everyone was indoors before running down the stairs with Valerie leading the way.

Tamara spoke first, "I can't remember the last time I saw this much drama in real life."

"Not even in the Kingdom," Laura said. "Annabella would be so—"

"Horrified," Barbara said.

Carole walked over and hugged Barbara. "I had no idea about David." She shuddered. "All those years, I listened to him preach about love, marriage, and doing the right thing. At the end of each service, he would invite Miranda on stage. I always thought they were the perfect couple. I even went to him for marriage counseling. Everyone did. We . . . I had no idea that he and Henry, uh, I don't know what that is—" Her eyes welled with tears as she reached for a napkin on the nearby table.

While Barbara had been shocked, she could only imagine how devastated Carole must feel. It was a betrayal, of sorts. Barbara didn't harbor any homophobic thoughts—her relationship with Mario and Nico was a solid one—but she was not comfortable with all the deception. A deception that must have been necessary if David and Henry wished to continue working in conservative evangelical circles.

Tamara and Laura were comforting Carole, while Valerie stood on the sidelines. The younger woman whispered in Barbara's ear, "I don't know if this helps, but I don't think the preacher is gay. Bisexual, maybe, but not gay."

Barbara nodded as she recalled the short-lived marriage to Pearl Grace and Henry's reference to the many Jezebels who had shamelessly pursued the charismatic preacher. David had allowed the behavior, perhaps even encouraged it. Unlike Henry and everyone else on Kendra's lawn, David had not been annoyed by Arabella's antics. If they had been alone, David might even have made a pass. David Ferguson was definitely attracted to women.

Barbara sighed. "Thank goodness, it happened here at Kendra's. I wouldn't know what to do if we were in Canada or somewhere else."

"That's easy enough," Valerie said. "Start with the drugs. Arabella needs to go cold turkey on the pot and anything else she is imbibing. Her human brain isn't fully developed yet, and she shouldn't be messing with it."

Barbara's eyes widened. This was the first she had heard of mermaid brain development. That would definitely explain Arabella's narcissism and impulsivity. *And what of her own brain? Did she have the brain of fifty-four-year-old? Or was her brain age closer to that of Arabella's?* She shuddered at the last thought.

Carole and the others were watching her closely. As they exchanged glances, Barbara sensed they were vacillating between leveling with her and sparing her a few necessary truths.

"Spill it," Barbara said as she clenched and unclenched her hands.

"It takes three years for the mermaid brain to catch up with the human body," Carole explained. She waved her hands to include the others. "During our first year on Earth, we behaved very impulsively and clung to the men in our lives. We weren't afraid to demand all those creature comforts they promised us, and when they didn't deliver, we didn't behave too well."

Tamara continued. "That's probably why most mermaid relationships don't last longer than a year or two. Not too many men can handle that steady flow of demands and keep a mermaid happy." She managed a smile. "The only relationship that has survived longer than two years is Belinda's."

Barbara recalled that early morning conversation with Paul. He had admitted that Belinda was hell on heels when she had first arrived. Unlike other human males, he had given in to all her demands and turned his own life upside down to please her. And so had Stewart, Barbara thought. Never in a million years did she think that Stewart would give up his charmed life in Chicago and relocate to a small town in Canada. Barbara wondered if he was having any second thoughts about that decision. She hadn't been able to read him at all. But then she had been distracted by Arabella's outrageous behavior. Behavior that was definitely beyond the norm for both humans and ex-mermaids.

Valerie cleared her throat. "We're not sure about your brain development. We asked Kendra, but she refused to discuss your situation."

While Paul had reassured her that she was the farthest thing from a narcissist, Barbara wondered about the other facets of her development. That thirty-year age increment had definitely affected her emotionally. She struggled with decision making, and she preferred to avoid rather than face unpleasant situations. Her confidence level was nowhere near Belinda's or Kendra's. *How long would it take for her brain to catch up?*

"Your situation is unique," Carole said. "I don't think that Kendra really knows what's up with your brain. It's too bad you don't have that Numbers Mermaid anymore. She could find out for you."

But she did have Lisa738, Barbara thought. Now would be a good time to reveal that information, but it suddenly felt awkward. The others, especially Valerie, might be upset. After all, they had all bared their souls and shared the most intimate of details during those intense retreat sessions.

While Barbara had talked openly about Annabella, Arabella and the men in her life, she still hesitated when it came to discussing her Bella perks. Valerie teased her about her elevated status, but she had belonged to a different Kingdom. Barbara suspected the other ex-mermaids from the Mediterranean Kingdom would not be overly thrilled with Annabella's generous offer of a five-year tablet and access to a fourth Specialist Skill.

Before Barbara could respond, she was distracted by the sound of footsteps on the stairs. Stewart smiled briefly at the ex-mermaids. "Sorry to interrupt, but I need a few words with Barbara."

Barbara followed him inside to Kendra's office.

CHAPTER 32

Stewart shook his head as he gave her a once-over. "I don't know what look you're trying to achieve, but it's certainly an interesting one."

Barbara couldn't wait to peel off the dress and give back the whole kit and caboodle to Valerie. That is, everything except the straw hat sitting in Henry's SUV. She didn't expect Nora or Henry to return it and hoped that Valerie wouldn't be too upset. "It's a church-lady look that I was trying out for the day."

"And how's that working for you?"

Barbara started laughing and Stewart joined in. From start to finish, it had been a trying day, but one that would be forever etched in memory. In spite of all the drama, she had dodged a major bullet. And for that she owed Arabella heartfelt thanks, something that she would never have considered possible until today.

Stewart raised an eyebrow. "I can't believe you even considered a relationship with the preacher and his—"

"Accountant," Barbara finished and burst into laughter again.

"That's a unique way of describing it." He gave her rueful smile. "And you didn't see it?"

"I wasn't looking for it," Barbara said softly. She had ignored those overwhelming scents that her Intuition had sent and had not listened when Kendra questioned the wisdom of a fling with the preacher. Instead, she had listened to Valerie who had encouraged her to pursue David. "Kendra knew," Barbara mumbled.

"I can't imagine a psychic missing that flag."

Barbara frowned. "Why didn't she say anything?"

"Would you have listened?"

Barbara shook her head wordlessly. Kendra knew she wasn't ready to face the truth so she had given Barbara space. That was Kendra's way. And all the while, Barbara had thought the older woman was taking distance.

Stewart cleared his throat. "While I find the many twists and turns of your love life interesting, we need to discuss another matter."

Arabella. The name no longer conjured up anxiety or stress. If anything, Barbara felt sorry for the beautiful woman who was single-handedly destroying all those wonderful advantages she had been given. And more importantly, Barbara no longer envied or feared her sister. While she was not prepared to have an intimate relationship with Arabella, Barbara would help in any way she could.

"I had a long chat with Kendra, who has agreed to help Arabella detox." Stewart paused. "This trip was really a last-ditch effort to preserve our marriage. Belinda called and persuaded me to give Arabella another chance. She thought that a change of scenery would rekindle the romance. And I went along with it. I should have suspected something when Arabella insisted on visiting the Grand Canyon. Belinda and I tried to persuade her to consider a Caribbean or Hawaiian cruise, but she wouldn't budge. Neither one of us realized she had another agenda." His lips tightened. "Arabella was fine on the flight and at dinner last night. And then, I got careless with my papers and she got nosy and discovered the new will I had signed last week. Everything went downhill after that."

Barbara raised her eyebrows. "Did you cut her out of the will?"

Stewart's laugh was a hollow one. "Hardly. She's

well provided for but not enough to compete with Belinda Armstrong."

"Not too many people can compete at that level," Barbara muttered.

Weariness crept into Stewart's eyes. "Well, that certainly won't be my problem after I'm gone. And I suspect that Arabella will quickly find a replacement." He sighed deeply. "I will fly back to Chicago tomorrow evening. Arabella will stay here for as long as it takes. And then, we'll sit down and have a long chat about this marriage."

Barbara suspected that Arabella had been indulging her every whim without giving any thought to possible consequences. A dangerous state of affairs for an addict. And, that's what her sister had become. So many questions whirled through Barbara's mind. *Where was Arabella getting her drugs? Had she involved any of the Cardeners? Why did Stewart let her drive when she was high?* The Stewart Tobin she had once known would never have been manipulated by a woman and let things reach this state.

Barbara chose her words carefully. "I'm surprised you were able to talk Arabella into detox."

Stewart managed a smile. "Kendra has excellent powers of persuasion. And I did promise Arabella a treat. Tomorrow, we're spending one last day together. She's hellbent on seeing the Grand Canyon and having what she likes to call a proper Last Supper before starting detox."

Don't go! The shout reverberated throughout Barbara's entire body. It was the first time she had felt these intrusive thoughts so viscerally and she was frightened, frightened for both Arabella and Stewart. She grabbed Stewart's arm. "Cancel it. Change your flight and leave tomorrow morning."

Stewart's eyes twinkled. "Is there a reason behind all this concern?"

"I don't have a good feeling about the two of you

spending tomorrow together." Barbara shivered. "What if she sneaks off and takes her drugs again?"

"Arabella promised that she would abstain from all drugs tomorrow. She emptied out the pharmacy in her purse and gave Kendra permission to go through her suitcase. And just in case, I'm returning the BMW and renting another car for tomorrow."

Barbara's eyes narrowed. "And talking about BMWs—"

Stewart held up his hand. "Arabella expressed an interest in black BMWs. I figured it was a genetic thing and humored her. Just to be clear, I didn't know you were here in Sedona. On the plane, she casually mentioned that she would like to visit Kendra. I didn't think it odd and hoped that Kendra would talk some sense into her." He pressed his lips together. "I would never, never have come here to torment you."

"Well, I'm glad you did. Arabella helped me dodge a bullet and for that I'm grateful."

"Would you really have pursued that preacher?"

"I was attracted to David but Henry . . . well, Henry was another story." She decided not to confide any details about David's past. As soon as she left Sedona, she would put all of this unpleasantness behind her. The only one she worried about was Nora. Barbara suspected that Nora must have had inklings about the relationship between her husband and David. And Miranda had probably known and accepted it as well.

Stewart glanced at his watch and frowned. "I'm meeting one of my clients for dinner in Phoenix." He cleared his throat. "Before I leave, I want to say that I'm sorry for any pain I may have caused. I was hurt by the way you ended our relationship, and I used Arabella to get back at you."

"Did you love her?"

"She reminded me so much of you, a younger more malleable you." He smiled wistfully. "At least, that's what I thought when I first met her."

Barbara smiled. "Hell on heels."

"And much more than I was prepared to deal with." He raised his eyebrows. "What about Graham?"

"Not really sure. I may try going solo for a while."

"I can't even imagine that happening." He leaned over and hugged Barbara tightly.

As soon as Stewart walked out the door, an immense sadness engulfed Barbara. She had wanted to say so much more to him. While he would be returning to pick up Arabella the following morning, Barbara doubted they would get any more one-on-one chats. And if Stewart and Arabella divorced, the chances of running into Stewart again were highly unlikely.

Email him. This time, she heeded the advice and headed toward her room. The other ex-mermaids had also retired to their rooms and were resting or preparing for the evening meal. Barbara groaned. She was still full from today's lunch. Nora's lovely lunch.

While Barbara was glad to be moving on, she still had misgivings regarding that calm and gentle soul who had created her own refuge in the Arizona outback. Barbara wondered if Nora would find comfort in it again. She could leave Henry and start over, but Barbara doubted that Nora had that kind of confidence. She had never worked outside the home and had probably never even written a check.

If she garnered the courage to divorce Henry, he would ensure that she walked away from the marriage with only the clothes on her back. Barbara's lips tightened. That was her one and only nagging regret. She would never see or hear from Nora again. It was too risky for Nora to attempt any contact without angering Henry. The fling, if you could call it that, had barely lasted a week and Barbara was more than happy to put this episode behind her.

After a quick shower, Barbara took out her laptop and composed an email.

To: Stewart
From: Barbara

I was so glad we finally had a chance to talk, but so much was still left unsaid. It may be a while before our paths cross, so I decided to write and express my feelings in this email.

I don't think I ever thanked you properly for taking me on as a client. Without your help and support, It's Your Time *would never have been published or achieved such high acclaim. And while I struggled with my feelings toward you, I know now that you genuinely cared for me and were willing to make a commitment. It was too soon and too rushed for me. I had been on Earth barely three months and still second-guessed all my decisions.*

I often wonder what would have happened if I had taken you up on your offer. Would we still be together? And more importantly, would we be happy together? Those two days we spent in Chicago were surreal, and I feared that once the magic dissipated you would tire of me. Or worse, I would never fit into your world. After being brutally transformed by Annabella and abandoned by Andrew, I simply could not face another rejection. I wanted a sure thing, a guarantee that my next relationship would be a safe and secure one. How ironic that I ended up being rejected once more, this time by Graham, the "safe" man.

Don't get me wrong. I still believe that Graham is the right man for me and I hope that we can resolve our differences. I also hope that you and Arabella can recapture the love you both experienced in Crete and during those first weeks in Carden. While I'm not one of her greatest fans, I realize now that she has her own issues, major ones from her mermaid days.

I'm glad to hear that Kendra has agreed to help.

Take good care of yourself.

Love,

Barbara

She hit 'send' and then took out the tablet. After hearing about the election on Saturday, Barbara had given Lisa738 her space. She knew the Numbers Mermaids would be putting in double shifts. In less than twenty-four hours, the election would be over and the results would be known. If Annabella were not re-elected, Barbara would have only a tiny window of time before the deadline for the fourth Specialist Skill expired.

Barbara decided not to wait that long. She tapped the green button and Lisa738 appeared. She appeared glad to see Barbara, but it was clear that she was in need of several nights of uninterrupted rest. Her usually well-groomed hair had been pulled back in a loose, untidy bun and there were noticeable bags underneath her bright-blue eyes.

Barbara touched the screen. "I'm sorry to bother you."

"I could use a break," Lisa738 whispered as she nodded to someone off the screen. "My supervisor has given me permission."

Barbara had assumed that Lisa738 reported exclusively to Annabella. It amazed her how little she had observed during her time in the Kingdom. Content to stay in the bubble that Annabella had created, Barbara had not had a single dealing with a Numbers Mermaid or merman. And without realizing it, Barbara had adopted Annabella's antipathy and snobbery toward anyone who wasn't a Bella or an Anna. While she still resented her grandmother for the brutal transformation, she was grateful for the changes it had wrought within her. Barbara treasured her relationship with Lisa738 and intended to savor the next five years.

"You must be counting the hours until this election is over," Barbara said.

"It has been one of the most grueling experiences. Annabella and the Inas are running neck and neck. It's too close to call."

Barbara breathed a sigh of relief. When they had spoken earlier in the week, Lisa738 had not sounded too confident about Annabella's prospects.

Lisa738 continued speaking. "Offering to train Rosanna and Leanna has made all the difference. We were all surprised to hear that Annabella was willing to relinquish her hold on the Kingdom when the two Annas reached the quarter-century mark. That was a strategic move on her part, and the mermaids and mermen are warming up to her again."

Barbara smiled but said nothing. She would let Lisa738 go on thinking it had been Annabella's decision.

Lisa738 frowned at Barbara's attire. "Are you ill?"

Barbara laughed. "No, I took a shower and decided to lounge around." She gave Lisa738 a quick summary of the day's events.

When Barbara finished speaking, Lisa738 lowered her voice. "I'm not surprised, but it saddens me to hear that an ex-mermaid could sink so low and in such a short period of time." She paused. "I won't share this information with Annabella until after the election. I don't want to distract her right now."

Barbara cleared her throat. "The other ex-mermaids were talking about our human brain development. They mentioned a three-year gap—"

"And you're wondering about your situation," Lisa738 finished. "I honestly don't know and neither does Annabella. When she added thirty years to your human age, she set a precedent, a dangerous one. The other elders were horrified and several of them made their feelings known throughout the Kingdom."

Barbara was surprised to hear there had been a backlash. While part of her was pleased to hear that Annabella's actions had triggered negative reactions, Barbara wondered if that would be held against her in tomorrow's election.

"Annabella and I worried about you at the start," Lisa738 confided. "But we decided not to share those concerns. Annabella monitored your activities very carefully during that first month. We both breathed sighs of relief when you picked yourself up. We knew that you would turn your life around. And sure enough you did." She winked. "Three men in less than a year."

Barbara winced. Despite all her career success, the mermaids in the Mediterranean Kingdom would focus primarily on the number of men in her life. Which at this point was a big fat zero.

Lisa738 frowned. "My supervisor is pointing to the break-timer. I only have a few minutes left. Is there anything you need?"

"Oh, yes. I'm sorry. I don't want you to get into any trouble. I've decided on my fourth Specialist Skill. I want Financial Acumen."

Lisa738 clapped her hands. "You're the first one to request that Skill, a Skill that will last with you long after I'm gone." She raised her eyebrows. "Do you know what you're getting with this Skill?"

"I'll be in the same ballpark as Warren Buffett, Donald Trump—"

Lisa738's voice became more animated. "You'll understand how money works and how to make it work for you. You will possess the ability to glance at a stock, mutual fund, land deal, or any other business proposal and quickly decide whether or not it is viable. You won't get into any financial difficulties, and you will be able to help others get out of bankruptcies and improve their net worth and bottom lines."

Barbara could easily visualize the seminars and workshops that she could now facilitate with ease and confidence. She was ready to move beyond the soft skills and help women conquer their fears and insecurities around money. Her first clients would be ex-mermaids.

"Are you ready?" Lisa738 asked. "Remember, you'll need to lie down for a while afterward." She pointed to the new button that had appeared below the screen.

Barbara picked up the button, peeled off the coating, applied it to her left temple, and waited for the unsettling sensation. This time, the experience was more intense. As Barbara lost her balance, she had to hold on to a nearby chair for support. As she watched Lisa738 fade away, she stretched herself out on the bed.

CHAPTER 33

When Barbara awakened, she was shocked to discover she had slept almost fourteen hours. Thinking back to her previous experiences with Specialist Skills, she couldn't recall spending so much time in bed afterward. But then yesterday's events had been stressful ones, from the initial drive with Henry to that final scene with Arabella.

As she reviewed each event, she found herself mentally thanking Arabella again. From the beginning, she had felt ill at ease with Henry and had ignored the strong messages her Intuition had sent. Those overwhelming floral scents had almost sickened her and if she had continued seeing David, that intensity would have become unbearable. Thoughts of David saddened her. She felt only immense sadness for his predicament. He would always feel obligated to please and appease Henry. And the next Mrs. Ferguson should be prepared to do the same.

The sadness was short-lived. Barbara couldn't believe how carefree she felt this morning. It was a feeling she had not experienced since leaving the Kingdom. While she had enjoyed and appreciated the launch of her book and its subsequent success, she had always been on edge. Keeping her mermaid origins a secret from Graham had prevented her from fully enjoying her new life. Arabella's arrival had broken Barbara open.

But that was all in the past. Barbara planned to sit down and have several conversations with Arabella before leaving Sedona. While they would never be BFFs, they could reach some kind of truce. They were mermaid sisters, and they should be able to live amicably. When Stewart divorced Arabella, Barbara would help the younger woman find her financial bearings.

With David out of the picture, Barbara was without a man in her life. Not necessarily a bad thing, Barbara thought as she showered and dressed for the day. After three days of dressing to please David, she found it refreshing to simply reach for her jeans and a Roots sweatshirt. She was looking forward to visiting Cathedral Rock Vortex and spending the day with Kendra and the other ex-mermaids.

As she made her way downstairs, she heard the hum of female voices in the kitchen. When she entered, they all clapped. Barbara felt herself reddening as she glanced around the room. She hadn't checked with Kendra regarding their departure time and from the glances that were exchanged around the room, she concluded that she was delaying them.

"Not to worry," Kendra said. "We don't have to be that structured today." She pointed to the buffet. "Take your time and have a proper breakfast."

Barbara helped herself to the scrambled eggs and fruit plate. She ignored the bagels and assortment of different breads. When she had put her jeans on this morning, they were snug around the waist. A sign that it was time to cut back the carbs and step up her exercise regimen.

"You missed more of the Bella drama," Tamara said as the others giggled.

"Arabella?" Barbara asked.

"She was all sugar and so sweet when she first got up. I figured she was putting on an act," Carole explained.

"And a pretty good one at that," Tamara said. "You would never know she was the same woman as that hellcat who terrorized us yesterday. She hugged everyone and was all lovey-dovey when Stewart arrived."

"How did you let that one get away?" Carole nudged Barbara. "He's a honey."

"And loaded," Tamara said, shaking her head. "With someone like that, you would be set for life."

Back to the money. If they weren't talking about men, they were talking about money and how to get more of it. Ideas were already percolating about possible seminars and workshops. Barbara couldn't wait to get back home and start planning her new life as a financial advisor.

She was ready to return to Cobourg via Vermont. She planned to have the long overdue conversation with Graham and ask for his forgiveness. Regardless of the outcome, she didn't want any bad feelings between them. Life was too short to hold grudges.

"I couldn't believe how upset she got about the Jeep," Valerie said. "And a high-end Jeep at that. Is she that attached to her precious BMW?"

Barbara's ears perked up. Arabella's change of mood could only mean one thing. She must have stashed drugs in the rental car. Barbara hoped that Stewart had found and disposed of the pot, cocaine, and whatever else Arabella was taking. It would be disastrous if someone at the rental agency discovered the drugs and decided to pursue the matter with the police.

As Barbara ate her eggs, she felt a strange sensation in her throat. The overwhelming stench of rotting meat overcame her as a frigid hand gripped her stomach. She pushed her plate away, covered her mouth, and ran quickly out of the room. She reached the powder room just in time and threw up. After heaving several times, she sank to the ceramic floor. Within seconds, she heard footsteps and felt a cool hand on her forehead.

"What did you smell?" Kendra asked.

"Rotting meat." Barbara faced Kendra. "Pork."

Kendra gasped. "One thing only. Death."

Arabella and Stewart are in danger. The intrusive

whisper sent chills up and down Barbara's spine. She forced herself to rise. "I must warn Stewart. I could call or email—"

"It's too complicated to explain over the phone." Kendra glanced at her watch. "They left about thirty minutes ago. If we hurry, we can catch up to them."

"Kendra, you've made plans for the day. I can't—" She was distracted by a sudden movement at the doorway. The ex-mermaids had gathered with their jackets and purses.

Carole spoke first. "If we take my van, we can catch up to that Jeep in no time."

"But what about the vortex?" Barbara asked.

The women laughed as Valerie approached and hugged her. "Honey, that vortex isn't going anywhere. But we are and we better hurry if we're going to catch up to your sister."

CHAPTER 34

When she had first seen Carole's Ford Explorer on Sunday, Barbara had wondered why a divorced sexagenarian with no children would need such a large vehicle. But it certainly came in handy today as Barbara stretched herself out in the back row with Valerie. No other vehicle could have accommodated all six women so comfortably. The women had split up in pairs: Carole and Kendra in the front, Tamara and Laura in the middle, and Valerie and Barbara in the back.

Carole appeared relaxed as she drove them to Flagstaff. All the angst she had demonstrated the previous Sunday had dissipated. She had also put yesterday's debacle behind her. In less than twenty-four hours, Carole would be leaving Arizona and David Ferguson behind.

Poor David. Barbara was certain that he would find a second wife, a third if you count his disastrous marriage to Pearl Grace. But that woman would have to accept Henry as part and parcel of their lives.

Valerie waved her hand in Barbara's face. "Are you daydreaming again?" She whispered, "I'm kind of glad we didn't visit that vortex. This is a lot more exciting."

Barbara raised an eyebrow. "You find this exciting?"

"I'm addicted to my soaps and actually taped fifteen hours' worth before I left." She winked. "But nothing could even come close to all this Bella drama. I could never in a million years have even imagined yesterday's scene. As for today . . . well, almost anything can happen."

Barbara flinched as she recalled Kendra's ashen face and startled eyes at the mention of rotting meat. Very little fazed

Kendra, but that troublesome omen had galvanized her into action. "I sincerely hope not."

"Stop worrying," Valerie said as she pointed toward Carole. "She's really gunning it today. We should catch up to them soon. And then Kendra can sweet talk Arabella out of whatever she is plotting."

"My sister can be pretty stubborn—"

"She's no match for Kendra. All Kendra has to do is hypnotize her again."

"Hypnotize her?" So, *that's* how Kendra had managed to get Arabella into the house so quickly. With her attention focused on David and Henry, Barbara had only a vague recollection of Arabella escorted by both Kendra and Stewart into the house.

"That's only one of the many tricks she has up her sleeve."

Barbara raised an eyebrow as she repeated. "Tricks up her sleeve?"

"Well, you know, Reiki, reflexology, past life regression. All that New Age stuff you read about. You name it, Kendra can call on it. That's her Specialist Skill." Valerie poked her. "I'm surprised you didn't follow her example."

"I admire Kendra but I couldn't visualize following in her footsteps."

"I guess you got more than you bargained for with Intuition."

"I certainly did," Barbara said. "And what Specialist Skills did you ask for?"

Valerie blushed. "Cuisine, Fashion Sense, and, uh, Dramatic Ability. I thought I could make it on the silver screen."

Barbara would not have considered such a Skill, but it made perfect sense for someone with Valerie's dramatic flair and desire to be center stage. And it did explain her extraordinary ability to ad lib. But in all their conversations, there had been no mention of any career, let alone an acting career.

Valerie leaned over and squeezed Barbara's arm. "Thanks for being so tactful. But I don't mind talking about my aborted acting career. When I first got the Skill, I was all gung-ho and even found an agent. But I quickly discovered the talent wasn't enough. At the time, I was living in a small town in Virginia and not willing to drive to Richmond or fly to New York whenever my agent called with a gig. I did get a few commercials but after my first sweetie left me, I was more interested in finding another man, and I let the dream go."

"But you still have the talent. Why don't you—?"

Valerie shrugged nonchalantly. "That ship has sailed."

Barbara couldn't shake the feeling that something very wrong was about to happen. To still her Intuition, she opened the window beside her and periodically leaned outside to breathe in the outside air.

While she enjoyed the tantalizing desert air, Barbara was ready for winter in Canada. She closed her eyes and imagined herself cross-country skiing in the conservation area behind their house in Cobourg. Sammy had offered to teach her snowboarding, and then she recalled with a pang that she probably wouldn't be seeing too much of him.

Barbara was startled out of her reverie by the sound of police and ambulance sirens. Carole pulled to the side as two police cars, an ambulance, and a fire truck whizzed by. When she merged back onto the road, Kendra said quietly, "Follow them, Carole."

Barbara's eyes filled with tears as she wrung her hands. If only she had awakened earlier, she could have tried to persuade Arabella and Stewart not to go. And now, now there would be collateral damage, or worse. Barbara longed to reach over and ask Kendra if she sensed anything. Kendra had probably foreseen exactly what would happen when Barbara described the stench. But as Kendra had pointed out many times, while her predictions had over ninety-five percent probability, there was still the issue of free will which could easily change the outcome of any event.

The van slowed down as they approached the scene of the accident. In addition to the emergency vehicles, there was a large Jeep and a U-Haul truck in the right lane. It appeared that both vehicles had been involved. The officer was signaling the traffic into the center lane.

"Pull to the right and park on the shoulder," Kendra said.

"I don't think he'll let me do that," Carole said.

"Let me deal with him," Kendra said. "Just stay in the van while I go out there and talk to him."

Valerie reached over and squeezed Barbara's hands. She leaned over. "Breathe."

Barbara was grateful she was surrounded by the other ex-mermaids. There was no way she could have dealt with this on her own.

CHAPTER 35

As Kendra walked toward the accident scene, the officer motioned for her to go back to the van. She continued, maintaining a slow but steady pace. After signaling two more cars, the officer walked purposefully toward Kendra. While Barbara couldn't make out his facial expressions or what he was saying, his body language relaxed as he approached Kendra. For most of the conversation, he nodded but when Kendra gestured toward Carole's van, he shook his head. After another brief conversation, they walked toward the stalled vehicles.

Carole faced the others. "This could take a while, ladies. So sit back and try to relax. I know it's hard, but—"

Tamara held up three DVDs and groaned. "*Star Wars, Terminator 2, Batman*. Not that I'm interested in watching anything, but what gives?"

Carole made a face. "Sorry! Thought I had gotten rid of all my ex's stuff. Any other suggestions out there?"

"I should have brought the DVD of my Elvis wedding," Laura said. "It's the best one yet."

"Which package did you pick?" Tamara asked.

"The Hound Dog Package," Laura replied.

"Isn't Elvis dead?" Barbara said as thoughts of her own aborted wedding came to mind. They had planned to exchange vows at City Hall and have a reception at the Carden Inn. Everything was tentative: the dress, menu, even the date. Graham had wanted to marry as quickly as possible while Barbara preferred to wait until the spring. Thankfully, no deposits had been made and no invitations had been sent.

"An Elvis impersonator walks the bride down the aisle and oversees the entire event," Laura explained. "You also get roses, a limo, DVD and, of course, Elvis songs. Some of the packages even include a reception."

"Where does all of this take place?" Barbara hadn't heard of any Elvis weddings in her circle. Most of the women at Eagle Vision were either married or divorced. Nico and Mario were gay and perfectly content to stay together without a marriage certificate. She suspected that Gillian and Andrew would eventually marry but not in an Elvis chapel. Gillian would want a large wedding and reception in Chicago.

"Las Vegas," Laura said. "Lots of Elvis Chapels on the main strip. You can find a wedding to match almost any budget. But the Hound Dog Package is the best deal at two hundred and seventy-five dollars."

Barbara couldn't resist asking. "How much for all the bells and whistles?"

"That would be the Elvis Unplugged and Plugged package," Laura replied. "You get more roses, more songs, and a reception for twenty-five people. It's over a thousand bucks."

Tamara frowned. "Why would you need a reception?"

"Enough about weddings," Valerie said as she squeezed Barbara's hand.

Barbara rewarded her with a grateful smile. She didn't want to hear any more wedding talk.

"I'd like to hear more about Stewart," Tamara said as the others nodded in agreement.

Barbara couldn't believe they wanted her to rehash her relationship with Stewart. Especially now, of all times. But as her eyes traveled from woman to woman, she realized that no malice was intended. They were genuinely curious and they also wanted to distract her. Barbara sighed. "What do you want to know?"

"How did you feel when you met him for the first time?" Valerie asked.

"He literally took my breath away," Barbara said dreamily as she recalled the strong, visceral reaction she had experienced in Gillian's Chicago condo. His expressive green eyes had immediately locked with hers and she found herself rendered speechless. All she could do was smile while she took in his beautiful features. "I can still remember what he was wearing that day. Jeans with boots and a brown sweater topped with a tan leather jacket. His collar was turned up."

"What else happened that day?" Tamara asked.

"We had brunch at The Signature Room in downtown Chicago. The place was teeming with people and it took forever to get to our table. He must have shaken hands with half the men in the room. As for the women, they were all trying to get his attention while ignoring me. One of the servers nearly dropped her tray of water glasses."

"I could see that happening," Laura said. "When did he make the first move?"

"Right after lunch. At Millennium Park. We were walking through the tree-lined promenade when he stopped and kissed me. When I reminded him about my relationship with Graham, he argued for a bit and then called the Omni to cancel the suite he had booked for the afternoon." Barbara smiled at the gasps and raised eyebrows.

"He had booked the suite before meeting you?" Carole whistled. "Talk about confidence."

Barbara explained, "I was shocked as well, but when I mentioned it to Gillian, she informed me that he puts up many of his clients at the Omni. He enjoyed courting women and giving them a taste of a more opulent lifestyle."

"Must be nice to be that loaded," Tamara muttered. "Did you receive any nice jewelry?"

"I got roses and a black BMW," Barbara replied.

"What?"

"You've got to be kidding!"

"A car. He gave you a car."

Carole's eyes narrowed. "How long had you been going out before you got that car?"

"We only went out twice in Chicago and then I went back to Carden. Before I left, he agreed to give me six months to decide whether or not I wanted to pursue a relationship with him. But he didn't wait six months. He started sending me roses almost immediately, but I put an end to that. I didn't want to alert Graham—"

"But Graham found out anyway," Valerie said.

"Stewart loved the chase, and he had to call the shots," Barbara explained. "When I returned to work in January, the owner of a nearby dealership visited and presented me with a beautiful bouquet of roses and the keys to a black BMW. All in full view of my colleagues and half the townspeople. When Graham found out, he was livid and left."

"What did you do?" Carole asked.

"I had to give up my position at ReCareering," Barbara said as her eyes welled with tears. While her boss had been sympathetic and suggested a short break until the gossip died down, she had been relieved when Barbara offered to leave. Thankfully, Sharon Clarke had taken her call and offered her a job at Eagle Vision.

"What about the car?" Tamara asked.

"I drove it for almost three months as I considered Stewart's offer." She felt herself reddening "But after meeting with Kendra, I realized that I needed to detach from the car." It had taken all of Kendra's persuasive powers to convince Barbara that she needed to buy her own car with her own money.

"What about the, um, did you—?" Carole stammered.

Valerie frowned. "For heaven's sake, we're all grown women here." She turned to Barbara. "How was the sex?"

Barbara closed her eyes as memories of that glorious

afternoon floated through her mind. "It was wonderful, simply wonderful."

"And yet you let him go," Tamara said.

"It's hard to explain," Barbara said. "There was a lot of passion, but we only had those two days together. I don't know—"

"They're coming," Carole said.

Barbara gasped at the sight of Kendra and the officer holding up Arabella. The younger woman appeared dazed, as if in a trance. So many questions whirled through Barbara's mind. Was Arabella high? Did Kendra hypnotize her? And most important of all . . . Where was Stewart?

CHAPTER 36

Kendra approached Tamara and motioned for her to move up to the front seat. With the officer's help, they carefully seated Arabella in the middle row. Kendra thanked the officer and climbed in beside Arabella.

In and out. In and out. Barbara focused on her breath. She kept her eyes down while clenching and unclenching her hands. Something terrible had happened to Stewart. She could feel it, but she didn't want to see it in Kendra's eyes. Not yet, anyway.

"What happened?" Carole asked.

Kendra spoke in a low voice. "Four young men were driving to Arizona State to furnish their new apartment with furniture from their parents' homes. The driver had never handled a vehicle of that size. When they reached a sharp curve in the road, he lost control and the vehicle slid into the right lane, slamming into Stewart's Jeep." Her eyes were brimming with tears. "Two of the young men and Arabella managed to jump out the passenger side and ended up with a few scrapes."

"What about the others?" Barbara asked in a small voice.

"The passenger on the driver's side in the U-Haul was rushed to the hospital in Flagstaff. The paramedics are confident he'll pull through." She paused. "The drivers didn't make it."

Heartache spread across Barbara's chest. She heard the gut-wrenching screams that pierced her very being. Who was making those godawful screams? Her eyes frantically searched the others, but all she encountered were pale, ashen faces and tear-filled eyes of concern. Barbara realized that she was screaming, screaming like she had never screamed before. Out of the corner of her right eye, she noticed movement beside her. When she looked up, she saw Kendra sitting next to her. While Barbara couldn't make out what Kendra was saying, she followed the older woman's finger and fixated on a gold medallion.

Barbara woke up to the most glorious sunrise, one she hadn't seen since leaving the Kingdom. Her lips curled up in a smile as she breathed in the ocean air. She was back in Malta. When she turned to her right, she was surprised to see three beaming mermaids sitting on a large rock, Annabella in the middle, surrounded by Leanna and Rosanna. Barbara smiled. Her grandmother had won the election.

The three mermaids floated over and took turns hugging Barbara. When she hugged Annabella, Barbara realized this was their first happy time together. Since leaving Malta, most of their conversations had been tense ones filled with tears, recriminations, and regrets.

Barbara congratulated Annabella and exchanged pleasantries with Leanna and Rosanna. The younger mermaids dominated the conversation, taking turns regaling Barbara with details about the election. For the first time, Annabella was content to stay in the background, smiling radiantly as her protégés outlined their plans for the Kingdom.

"Annabella will always have a special place in our hearts and in our homes," Leanna said as she squeezed the older mermaid's hand. She smiled at Barbara. "We will visit you often."

Rosanna continued. "When we procreate, Annabella will be an honorary grandmother. And we will also share our daughters with you, Barbara. You will be their honorary aunt."

Barbara noted the use of the plural pronoun but said

nothing. Leanna and Rosanna were already planning the future, one where Annabella would no longer be chief elder. Barbara was very happy with the outcome of the election and knew that Annabella would be well taken care of by both Leanna and Rosanna.

Leanna and Rosanna exchanged glances and then floated over to another rock. Annabella waited until they were out of earshot before speaking to Barbara. "I heard about Stewart's death."

Barbara's eyes brimmed with tears. For a short while, she had thought of it as a bad dream, one that would disappear once she woke up in the morning. But it wasn't a dream. She would never see Stewart again. Barbara tried but could recall very little of the previous day's events. The stench of rotting meat. The drive to Flagstaff. And that gold medallion swinging back and forth. Kendra must have hypnotized her. But that seemed so long ago. What time was it? If it was dawn in Malta, it must be late evening in Arizona. She tried to do the math, but her brain wouldn't co-operate.

"Kendra called Belinda and Paul," Annabella said as she wrapped her arms around Barbara.

Barbara wondered what else had happened. Her brain felt like a big fuzz ball. *Had Kendra hypnotized her?* She would find out soon enough. In the meantime, she managed a smile for her grandmother. This was a victory for Annabella, one that needed to be savored and appreciated. "I'm glad everything worked out for you. You will be able to retire with dignity."

Annabella nodded in the direction of the Annas. "They'll do a good job. I'm so glad you persuaded me to take them on. It made all the difference." She spoke more briskly. "What are your plans?"

One thing, Barbara knew for sure. She would not be staying too much longer at Kendra's house. While the animosity toward Arabella had dissipated, she didn't feel comfortable and Barbara doubted that her sister would appreciate her presence in the house while she was going through rehab. Kendra would devote all her time and energy to helping Arabella and would not want any other distractions.

As Barbara shifted her position on the rock, heavy fabric fell from her shoulders. She looked down and smiled in appreciation at the colorful quilt that had been draped around her shoulders. It was her quarter-century quilt. During her years in the Kingdom, she had often visited the small group of Ettas, who were working on the quilt that would be presented to her during her quarter-century celebration. Barbara stood and spread the quilt on the rock. She lovingly traced the images that had once been so familiar. Isabella as a baby mermaid on her grandmother's tail. Isabella playing with Rosanna and Leanna. Isabella on her twenty-first birthday. All surrounded by beautiful coral, jellyfish, and sea critters. When she left the Kingdom, she had assumed that work on it would stop.

Annabella smiled. "They've been working on it, day and night, during the past week. I wanted to make sure that you would get it, whatever happened."

The tears flowed freely as Annabella and Barbara embraced.

Annabella regained her composure. She adjusted the quilt, draping it gently over Barbara's shoulders. "This quilt was intended to celebrate a milestone. I had hoped that milestone would have been your quarter-century party. Your wedding night will have to do."

"That day may never come."

"Don't give up hope," Annabella said. "It can happen."

Barbara managed a tight smile but said nothing.

Annabella smiled knowingly. "Be patient." She kissed Barbara on both cheeks and floated back toward Leanna and Rosanna.

CHAPTER 37

Barbara awakened to the persistent ringing of the telephone on her night table. Groaning, she picked it up and was greeted by Kendra's soft voice. "Good morning, Barbara. The others will be leaving in about an hour's time. I thought you might want to say your goodbyes." Before Barbara could respond, Kendra hung up the phone.

Barbara leaped out of bed. She took a quick shower, applied minimal makeup and got dressed. As she descended, she heard the hum of voices and subdued laughter emanating from the kitchen. When she entered the kitchen, Valerie rushed over and hugged her tightly. Barbara would definitely miss her afternoon conversations with the younger woman. But she was determined not to lose touch. Emailing and texting would have to do until they met again.

Carole, Tamara, and Laura took turns hugging her until Maria yelled, "Let her eat her crepes!"

Everyone laughed good-naturedly. They were used to Maria's admonishments about eating food as soon as it was prepared. Whenever any of them dawdled over their food or were distracted by conversations, she would shake her head crossly. If it wasn't hot, it simply wasn't good enough. As Barbara bit into her crepe, she sighed contentedly. All those lovely berries—raspberries, blackberries, strawberries, blueberries—that were definitely fresh and not frozen. In her mind, she quickly itemized all the other ingredients: sour cream, milk, vanilla. Her Specialist Skill for Cuisine came in handy whenever she encountered a food she particularly liked.

As Barbara's eyes traveled around the room, she lingered on each woman, recalling the issues they had discussed during the first two days of the retreat. For Carole, Tamara, and Laura, money was the primary source of their discontent. They didn't have enough to live the lives they felt they should be living. And according to Carole, they were no longer attracting the right calibre of men into their lives. Divorced men came with baggage they were not prepared to accommodate. Difficult stepchildren. Aging parents. Dwindling bank accounts. With the exception of Valerie, they weren't attracting younger men.

But Kendra had worked some of her magic. During their evening dinners and game sessions, Barbara had heard scattered comments about new diet and exercise regimens and possible volunteer activities. No mention of employment of any kind. Or developing improved money management skills. There was definitely a demand for her services as financial counselor. But this wasn't the time to bring that up.

As Barbara sipped her tea, she breathed in the most delightful scent of roses. Not at all intense like the floral medley that had assaulted her earlier in the week. But it wasn't a new smell. She had breathed in this lovely aroma the morning of the day Graham had proposed. What a wonderful day that had been—her most perfect day on Earth. *But how could that perfection even be replicated?* Graham was thousands of miles away and there was no other man on the horizon.

"Earth to Barbara!" Valerie was waving frantically as the other women laughed. "You're daydreaming again."

Barbara smiled at Valerie. Young and beautiful Valerie who appeared not to have any major issues with men or money, but there was definitely something lacking in her life. Barbara suspected that her aborted theatrical career contributed to her occasional bursts of melancholy.

"We were wondering if you'd like to meet up with us in the summer," Valerie said. "I'm hosting in Albuquerque."

Barbara nodded enthusiastically. "Of course."

Tamara pointed to the clock. "We need to leave now if we're going to make those flights."

The women swung into action. Everything had been preplanned so they could leave together. Carole would drive Tamara and Laura to the airport and then head home while Valerie drove north to New Mexico. Barbara followed the women to their cars. More hugs and promises to keep in touch were exchanged.

Barbara stood on the front steps, waving and blowing kisses to the departing women. Barbara noticed Kendra's Jeep in the driveway and realized the older woman had been nowhere in sight during the leave-taking. Even more surprising, no one had commented on her absence. There must have been some kind of emergency or crisis that Kendra was forced to deal with and, of course, the ex-mermaids would have understood.

As soon as she entered the house, Kendra emerged from the living room. "Belinda and Paul are here."

"When did they arrive?"

"An hour ago."

Barbara took a deep breath and headed toward the living room. As soon as she opened the door, Belinda ran toward her. She hugged her tightly and started sobbing. "I'm so glad to see you. I've missed you so much. I can't begin to say . . . I'm so sorry."

Barbara gently untangled Belinda's arms and gasped as she examined her mother's face. They had been apart for less than two months, but Belinda was already showing signs of accelerated aging. There were wrinkles around her expressive green eyes and lips. Her skin seemed to have lost its luster and several white hairs peeked through her usually well-coiffed and perfectly colored auburn hair.

Before Barbara could speak, Paul approached and hugged her. "So sorry, kiddo." There was a grayish cast to his face and his cheekbones appeared more prominent than before. The coming of Arabella had affected all of them.

Barbara sat in the armchair opposite them and watched as Belinda sobbed quietly in a large man's handkerchief. What surprised Barbara was that Paul was not comforting Belinda or even sitting close to her.

"We came as soon as we heard," he said in a deadpan voice.

Belinda gazed imploringly at Paul, but he ignored her, maintaining eye contact only with Barbara. They had been arguing. Something Barbara had never seen before. She was realistic enough to know there must have been disagreements throughout their twenty-four-year marriage. No relationship could survive that long without some disharmony. But Barbara suspected that any previous tiffs had blown over quickly.

She smiled at both of them. "Thank you for coming. I'm better today, but I suspect I won't do so well at the funeral."

Paul's lips tightened. "We've been advised to stay away."

Barbara gasped. "What!"

"When Kendra called Stewart's brother," Paul explained, "he made it clear that Arabella and her clan were not welcome to attend. I suspect he said more, but Kendra tactfully left it at that."

Barbara would have liked to pay her last respects, but she would not intrude on Stewart's family. Especially his elderly parents who must be grief-stricken. They certainly didn't expect their youngest son to predecease them.

Paul motioned toward the back terrace where Arabella was sprawled on one of the loungers. "She did a number on him, and I suspect his family knows about all her shenanigans."

"That's not fair!" Belinda said tearfully. "She's still adapting."

"Still adapting!" Paul roared as he glared at Belinda. "Is that what you call tormenting a sister, destroying a man's livelihood, and nearly breaking up two marriages? And that's just for starters. God only knows what other stunts she tried to pull over Stewart."

Belinda's eyes flashed with anger. "Whatever she did, she's paying for it now. She could barely get out of bed this morning. She's mourning. I can tell she's sincere."

"About as sincere as a three-dollar bill." Paul glared at Belinda. "I'm glad she's not coming back with us. She needs to stay here for a while, a long while."

"Three months," Belinda said as she waved her hands. "And she'll be paying a pretty penny for all this help."

"Do you want me to find her a less-expensive place?" Paul's jaw hardened. "Lots of places in Upstate New York and Ontario that'll give her a strong dose of tough love."

Belinda shuddered. "How can you even suggest that? She can't go into regular rehab."

"Well, then she's got to pay the price for fancy mermaid rehab." He muttered, "He's left her enough money for that."

Fresh tears swelled in Belinda's eyes. "Kendra's fees will eat up almost all her allowance."

How wise of Stewart not to give her a lump sum. Having listened to the other ex-mermaids describe their early shopping sprees, Barbara believed that Arabella could easily follow their example and end up destitute.

"Not *my* problem," Paul said. "If she can't survive on ten thousand dollars a month, I have no sympathy."

Barbara painfully recalled her own circumstances a year ago. All she had received was a check for ten thousand dollars and that money was supposed to last an entire year. Granted, she did have a rent-free apartment, but those first few months had been very stressful ones.

"Stewart didn't leave her any property," Belinda said. "She doesn't have a home of her own." Her eyes silently implored Paul to offer shelter. In addition to their apartment in Manhattan, Paul owned a summer house in Maine, and a *pied-á-terre* in Toronto.

"Not *my* problem," Paul repeated.

Belinda started sobbing again, this time more loudly. Paul got up and left the room.

Barbara went to sit next to Belinda. She comforted her mother and waited until the sobs subsided. Belinda spoke first. "He's been like this for weeks. I've never seen him so angry and so upset. He barely looks at me and finds every excuse to leave the house. I can't begin to tell you how unbearable those five hours on the plane were."

Barbara wondered what event had triggered the quarrel. There were so many shenanigans to choose from, but she decided not to pursue that line of questioning. She was, however, curious about the twenty-four years of little or no marital strife. "You must have had arguments, disagreements in the past."

"If there was a mild disagreement, it lasted a day, two at the very most." Belinda grimaced. "I still remember that two-day freeze when I threatened to leave him if he didn't move his business to New York."

Forty-eight hours. That's all the time it had taken Paul Armstrong to forgive his wife for the outrageous suggestion to up-end his life. Any other man would have shown her the door.

"You think I'm spoiled, don't you?" Belinda's voice came out small and childlike.

"I think you were very fortunate in your choice of mate," Barbara amended. "And you still are. Paul doesn't hold grudges. I think this will blow over. Maybe not as soon as you would like, but he will come around." She hugged her mother. "I'll help."

"After all that Arabella and I put you through—"

"All is forgiven," Barbara said, and she meant it. While she wouldn't forget the outrageous stunts that Arabella had pulled, Barbara was willing to move on. As for Belinda, well, Belinda was mother to both of them. Barbara suspected it was much easier to be a mother to twenty-four-year-old Arabella who shared many of Belinda's interests.

Belinda gazed outside. "She's so different from . . . from you, from us. Those years on Crete hardened her, made her so bitter and untrusting. She was abused and used, never loved." She lowered her voice. "All because of those dark eyes."

Those dark pools were not all that unusual on Earth. People of color had eyes like that. And so did Valerie. But Valerie's eyes were full of light and the occasional mischievous glint. "Kendra will help her."

"I'm not too thrilled with Kendra's exorbitant rates, but I am happy that Arabella has agreed to stay. She needs help that I cannot give her. And I need a break from her." Belinda managed a smile as she squeezed Barbara's hand. "What about the other Armstrong man?"

Barbara shrugged. "Nothing on that front. And I'm fine with that for now."

"Just don't get too comfortable being alone," Belinda said. "It's not the life you were destined to live." She took out her compact and grimaced. "I need a major overhaul." She got up, kissed Barbara, and left the room.

CHAPTER 38

Barbara opened the sliding doors and went outside to join her sister. Arabella's appearance also shocked Barbara. Her long wavy tresses had been pulled back into a tight ponytail that exposed her well-chiseled features. She wasn't wearing any makeup at all and while there were no wrinkles or other visible flaws, her complexion lacked any luster. Her eyes were red-rimmed and swollen.

Barbara sat next to Arabella. She reached over and gently squeezed the younger woman's arm.

Arabella managed a smile as she put down her coffee cup. "Now I know what it takes to get your attention."

"And what's that?"

"Looking and feeling like crap."

Barbara laughed spontaneously and Arabella joined in. "Let's hope Paul doesn't hear us. He'll condemn me even more than he has since, well . . ." Arabella blushed and stammered.

"We don't have to talk about Stewart if you're not feeling up to it."

"No, I mean . . . that's not it. I've been in Paul's black books for a while now. Ever since you left Canada."

Barbara thought back to that last telephone conversation with Paul. He had sounded weary and impatient, but perhaps Barbara had misread the situation. She had assumed he was siding with Arabella and anxious to have Barbara take distance. *Why hadn't he tried to contact her?* So many other questions whirled through her mind, but there would be time later to have that conversation with Paul.

Barbara smiled at her sister. "I'm glad that you're staying here for a while. Kendra will help you."

Arabella yawned. "I guess."

Barbara was reminded of clients who had reluctantly agreed to treatment or therapy. In almost all cases, the results were less than spectacular. And if Arabella were going anywhere else, she would probably experience the same results. But Kendra was different. As the other ex-mermaids often joked, she was relentless. Barbara leaned over and grabbed Arabella's hands. "She will help you beat those addictions."

Arabella made a face. "I'm not that addicted." She snapped her fingers. "If I want, I can stop just like that. But I'll stay for the month."

Barbara chose to say nothing. Her sister faced a difficult battle ahead, one that would take her to her breaking point. One month would not be enough. While Barbara wasn't an expert on drug abuse, she predicted that Arabella's stay could easily extend to six months. And afterward, she would have to rebuild her life again.

You can help. She smiled at the intrusive thought. Yes, she would help, but she would be very careful not to offer too much and too soon. Thankfully, Kendra would be there to advise her.

"Did your friends leave?" Arabella gestured toward the kitchen. "It sounded like you had a great week together."

"Yes, yes we did." Barbara wondered how long Arabella had been sitting outside. "You could have joined us."

"They're your friends, not mine." Arabella lowered her gaze. "I don't make friends that easily. I'm not like you."

"You don't have to be like me to make friends," Barbara said softly.

"But it helps," Arabella said. "It helps to be one of the perfect Bellas and have Grandmother always looking out for you. Life would have been a lot easier without Aunt

Sarabella and her mean-spirited daughters harassing me. I had no one and you had everyone. Leanna and Rosanna never left your side. The other mermaids praised you. The mermen respected you and would never even think of touching you inappropriately." Tears spilled onto her cheeks. "Even here on Earth, they all favor you and not me."

Barbara hoped her eyes did not betray her. From Annabella and Belinda, she had learned that Arabella's life on Crete was a difficult one, but Barbara was horrified to hear just how alone and tormented her sister must had felt. No wonder she had trust issues. Barbara tried again. "Stewart loved you and Belinda still does. And I'm sure you made other friends—"

"I don't think you can count Ben and Sammy. Or the rest of that Eagle Vision crew. I was bored to tears every day at that place. No excitement at all."

"So, you had to create your own." Barbara's lips tightened as visions of Arabella and Ben having sex in her office came to mind.

"It was only that one time. And he was more than willing."

Barbara forced herself not to imagine that particular scene. "He's married with a family. Did you stop and consider the consequences of him losing *his* job?"

Arabella laughed bitterly. "You'll be happy to learn that Sharon has a double standard when it comes to employee misconduct. The women get suspended or fired, but the men get a slap on the wrist and a transfer."

While Barbara didn't approve of different standards for men and women, in this case, she was glad to hear that Ben had not lost his livelihood.

"What about you?" Arabella asked. "When are you going back to Eagle Vision?"

"I'm not going back." There would be time later to reveal details about her financial counseling business.

Arabella raised an eyebrow. "Sharon and the others would welcome you back with open arms. You're still their golden girl."

"Not interested."

"But what will you do?"

"I'll just putter for a while. Work on my next book and maybe pen a few articles." Barbara recalled Arabella's announcement about writing erotica but decided not to bring it up. She suspected it was another feeble attempt to attract attention.

"I guess you'll be searching for Number Five," Arabella teased.

Barbara was grateful for the change of subject. "I'm perfectly content to stay on my own for a while."

Arabella gestured toward the sliding doors. "Not going to happen."

Barbara followed her gaze. Graham was standing there.

CHAPTER 39

Arabella picked up her coffee cup and headed toward the other side of the house. Graham waited until she disappeared before coming out onto the patio. His face was unshaven and it looked like he had slept in his clothes all night. His hazel eyes flashed angrily as he moved the lounger and pulled up one of the other chairs. Barbara followed all his movements, keeping her gaze focused on his beautiful hands.

They sat quietly for a while, avoiding each other's glances.

Finally, Graham spoke. "I'm sorry about Stewart. I know that you and . . . um . . . well, it must have been hard for you . . . in spite of . . . ." His lips tightened as he waved toward the side of the house. He couldn't bring himself to say Arabella's name. And that was understandable.

Barbara smiled but maintained her distance. "Thanks, Graham. The day before he died, we had a nice chat and reconciled our differences. If he had lived, I would have been fine with seeing him and Arabella occasionally."

"I don't think that marriage would have lasted much longer."

Barbara recalled the anguish in Stewart's voice. He knew it was over, but he was still willing to let the relationship end on a graceful note. He had probably planned a lovely dinner where he would gently release Arabella. That had been Stewart's modus operandi during his bachelor days. He always broke it off gently and tried to remain friends afterward. Outside of Gillian, Barbara hadn't met any of his past loves, but she suspected they all hung onto that olive branch hoping, beyond hope, that he would have a change of heart and reconcile with them. Her eyes welled with tears at the thought of never seeing Stewart again. While she didn't know the funeral details, she suspected the church would be overflowing with family, friends, clients, and women who had loved and cherished Stewart Tobin. He would be missed.

Barbara took several deep breaths and focused on the man sitting in front of her. "How was Vermont?"

"I couldn't wait to get away from there." He added, "I won't be returning. Ever."

"What about your students?" Barbara couldn't believe he was reneging on his responsibilities as instructor. In the past, he had stayed until the end of each session and maintained regular contact with his students. He had even featured their artwork when he owned The Art Shoppe in Carden.

"One of my former students visited last week. I persuaded him to finish teaching the course. He needed the cash, and I needed to get away." He paused. "I was packing up when Dad called."

Barbara's heart beat faster. "Where were you planning to go?

"Cobourg." Graham made direct eye contact with Barbara. "I want to try again, but this time, no more secrets." Weariness crept into his voice. "So, if there's anything else you wish to share—"

Barbara smiled. "No more secrets."

He moved closer to her. "We still have one more issue to resolve. Arabella." His jaw tightened. "I don't want her in our lives."

Gwen had suffered at Arabella's hands and it would be a long time before she could forgive and let go. Gwen Scott was her father's daughter, through and through. Barbara suspected that she would also receive a dose, albeit a weaker one, of the same treatment. But Barbara was prepared to start at ground zero with Gwen.

Barbara's thoughts circled back to her family. Belinda and Arabella. That's all that remained of the Bella tribe on Earth. As Paul's wife and Graham's mother-in-law, Belinda would continue to be a part of their lives. The storm that she was presently experiencing with Paul would blow over. Of that Barbara was certain.

Arabella was another story. While she wasn't sure what type of relationship she wanted with Arabella, Barbara knew that she wanted to see her sister. "Arabella's made a lot of mistakes and so have I. In no way am I justifying her behavior and I doubt that we'll ever be close, but we can make an effort to be civil." She swallowed hard. "I don't expect you to get involved, but I will not abandon her."

Graham raised his eyebrows but said nothing.

"How's Gwen doing?" Barbara asked.

"She let Sammy back into the house. They're getting counseling and really working hard to make a go of it. They're expecting."

"When is the baby due?"

"April." He smiled widely. "I'll be a grandpa for the first time." He leaned over and kissed Barbara. "And you'll be a Grandma . . . Nana . . . Granny . . . Glamma . . . What's the mermaid equivalent?"

"Grandmother."

"Too formal. And it doesn't suit you at all." He gave her the once-over. "I think Glamma might do the trick. You're too young and gorgeous for all those other monikers." He reached into his pocket and pulled out a small box.

When Barbara opened the box, her eyes sparkled with delight at the beautiful emerald mermaid ring. Her hand trembled as she tried it on the third finger of her right hand.

"No, not that hand." Graham took it off and slid it on the third finger of her left hand. He whispered in her ear, "I don't think I can wait much longer."

Barbara's heartbeat quickened. "We'll be in Cobourg soon enough." Her mind raced forward and started planning the week's agenda. Fly out tomorrow. Unpack and rest on Tuesday. Maybe next week, they could go to City Hall.

Graham's eyes twinkled mischievously. "How about hopping over to a wedding chapel in Las Vegas?" He glanced at his watch. "If we leave now, we could be there for dinner and—"

"Elvis. I want Elvis to marry us." She raised her voice above Graham's roar of laughter. "The Hound Dog Package, if you can get it."

585008